I DREAM OF ZOMBIES

ZOMBIES

Zombiology Book 1

IMOGENE NIX

LOVE BOOKS

ISBN 978-0-6484841-5-8

This one is for Charlotte. She's been asking me for years to write a zombie story and while I wrote The Reset (which is the introduction to the series) this one is written with her in mind. Also for Scott and Shelby cause, you know… ideas!
Thanks also to Suzi, Keri and Sassie (my buds) and Tara for the awesome cover.
Thank you to Mark & Beth and even Mr Patrick (haha! See you're now included in the into!)
Remembering Teddy (my awesome little fluffy writing buddy who passed away earlier this year) along with Galilee (Mr Boofy Pants) and Cocoa!
Lastly, as always, thanks to you readers. Without you, there'd be no reason to write.

Imogene Nix
2019

Chapter 1

Julia

EVERY BONE ACHED. *Every. Single. One.*

The narrow bunk in my quarters cradled me with a squeak and a groan as I settled. I sighed and let my body relax as I tugged the single blanket over me.

Closing my eyes was always a trial as the memories I worked hard to keep at bay flooded my mind.

Blood. Screams. Reaching, grasping fingers.

Always the same.

I lay there and concentrated on sunshine, but within minutes I began to toss and turn. At one point I even tried counting sheep. As usual, nothing worked, and after a long while I clambered off the cot and rose.

My boots waited just over the edge, and I tugged them on.

Giving a heartfelt sigh, I headed for the door. The one clean shirt hanging on a peg was disregarded. After all, there was no need to dress up to be in public.

"Everyone looks the same these days," I muttered.

I wrenched the door open and made my way down the long,

industrial-green hallway toward the mess area.

Echoes of voices wafted on the air as I hurried toward the benchtop that held large carafes of water.

I poured a drink and scanned the information board. I checked the news written in cramped handwriting on the paper hanging there, dated this morning.

Specialist Team Required. Northlands region. Six to eight well-trained personnel to undertake extraction and retrieval. Enquire at Control Office from 0700 today.

Huh. I wonder who's there and why they need extraction?

Intrigued, I swiveled and craned my head, seeking others I knew and could trust for intel.

No one in these times would willingly take on a mission without knowing who and what they were facing. And given some of the ones currently here at the hospital camp, I needed to be picky if I wanted to survive.

Casey, a fellow female guard, stood at the long, metal benchtop, stirring the meal currently on offer. We all took turns assisting in the kitchen, clean up, and even burial details. I was one who couldn't cook, so they insisted I wash up, serve, or collect the dirty plates. It suited me to perfection though. Casey was more a hands-on kind of girl and had taken to the whole 'everyone mucks in' well and was taking lessons on basic cooking.

Since the onset of the plague—as we called it—no one worked regular hours. Those who'd survived and made their way to the various encampments were grateful for human company, food, and a secure roof over their head. Canberra alone had at least a dozen camps that I knew of. The most successful one was in an area far removed from here. I'd seen some pictures and talked to those from there but hadn't ever had the opportunity to meet up with the leaders, Liam and Elaine.

Our own camp was at least reasonably self-sufficient. In the early days, those who could travel and had farm animals and growing skills were highly sought after. They didn't take on guard duties either, their contribution deemed far too valuable for that.

Then there were the few with families, not that many of them had survived. They'd been sequestered to high-security areas in the middle of the camps, and the level of security clearance needed to get to those areas was deemed above my paygrade. At least that was the case here in Queanbeyan.

From day to day and week to week I rarely saw a child now.

The memory of my little sister dropped into my mind, and I swallowed hard. The loss that permeated every time I thought of her and my mother never seemed any less painful. My stepfather, Allan, had survived. To this day the acid burn of anger roiled in my gut, because my mind said it was wrong that he'd come out alive, yet my entire family was gone.

Allan had left the camp well over a month ago and hadn't returned. I didn't know where he'd gone—it wasn't like communication between us was a thing—but the fact that he'd left without even saying goodbye spoke volumes to me about our relationship.

He'd abandoned his wife and daughter to the tender mercies of...

"Forget it. Time's passed." But the bitterness in my voice never abated when I had this argument with myself.

I marched swiftly in Casey's direction.

"Hey. What's that?" I inspected the thick, gray mass she kept moving in the pot.

"Oatmeal."

It didn't look like anything I'd ever eaten before. No chunks of oat or creamy, white consistency here. I tugged my gaze away. "Know anything about the retrieval mission?"

She cocked an eyebrow. "Maybe."

Casey wasn't a woman of many words, but her shrewd blue gaze was likely weighing up whether I was going to see the camp commander. "And?"

"I don't know a lot. Someone who once held a senior position in the government went out on a mission and got stuck. Needs an urgent extraction along with some survivors. That's it."

"Hmm. It says Northlands."

"You're from that way, aren't you, J?"

I nodded absently. I usually avoided Northland missions, but maybe this was what I needed to clear the remnants of grief from my mind.

"Gonna put your name down?"

I shrugged. It didn't pay to do much more than that, otherwise it would be around the base quicker than the blink of an eye.

Leroy
0700

The clock ticked over the hour, and I blinked once, twice. Just checking in case my tired eyes read it wrong. Since I'd seen the notice on the board, I'd been waiting for the time to click by. Slowly. Right now, my backside felt numb as I swilled the last of the coffee in the mug in my hands. It was rough and black. I doubted I'd ever get used to that.

I'd only been at this base for a handful of days. Hanging around one base or another meant making acquaintances, and often that led to friendship. More than once, it had also led to connecting with other humans who died, and I wasn't going to make that mistake again.

These days my best and only friends were the gun in my holster and the rifle I carried. I placed the rifle beside me with an audible sound. *Clunk.*

I pushed the mug back and rose, the leather of my fingerless gloves rubbing at the webbing between my fingers as I stretched them out and back again.

"Finished?" the shrewd woman who'd been making the coffee—Casey I think she called herself—asked.

"Yeah." I attempted to avoid her gaze while I scanned the room filled with the misfits and detritus of humanity. "Where's the Control Office?"

She sniffed and indicated the hallway to the left.

"Thanks," I flung over my shoulder as I marched in that direction.

Team patrols might be the norm, though my experience was that this was an unusual request. Extraction. That hinted of enemy engagement, which was about the high point of my life. Not that I expected my life would be long.

It was all there was now to look forward to, wasn't it, though?

I smiled thinly.

Before the door sat several chairs. All of them full. Against the wall lounged a group of people. It seemed that the notice had brought out a range of interested people—among them, me. I sauntered over and rested my hip on the concrete wall, acting nonchalantly, and let the rifle settle on my shoulder as I summed up those waiting.

Three men, weary looking with a droop to their mouth. Likely veterans dismayed at the turn their lives had taken.

Two women huddled together, not talking but obviously comfortable with each other. One had tightly bound, red-gold hair, maybe late twenties, and high cheekbones. The other one was older and appeared to be well-seasoned. Both of them looked at me briefly before turning back to face the wall. The others were a motley assortment of younger men and women of various ages and physiques, but these ones captured my interest.

Most of the younger men were brawny with close-shaven hair. They all wore similar clothing: the ubiquitous camouflage which had become the norm after the spread of the virus, or *plague* as many called it.

Before I could engage any in conversation, the door opened and an older man, clearly with a military background, if his bearing and air were anything to go by, invited us inside.

He grunted as the last of us entered the room, then he shut the door forcefully and turned to us.

"Interesting crew. Matthews, Jones, and Forster, you're not going to be completing this mission."

The three elder men, the ones I'd tagged as vets, opened their mouths, but the man in charge raised a hand.

"I need you here, training the youngsters who are almost ready to hunt."

They muttered but took seats at the back of the room, the skin around their mouths tightening. Clearly they felt their usefulness in the field would be a better use of their skills.

"Madderns, you're needed here too. I need you to work with the younger girls. They need immediate training in self-defense. The older boys are getting restless, and there's too much interest in the girls right now for me to dismiss the growing problems there."

The older woman gave a curt nod and moved to the seats at the back of the room.

"Now, I know most of you, except..." The look he shot in my direction should have sent my spine tingling with alarm, but instead I raised my chin and eyed him off.

"I'm Leroy."

"And you're new here, aren't you, son?"

Hmm. A hard-ass wannabe military type. "Yes, sir. I've been moving between bases from Townsville through to here. I arrived in Quean-beyan five days ago, and I'm looking for a place on your team."

His eyes narrowed on me, as if trying to read my reasoning.

"You need to earn your place. I need six to eight well-seasoned people. Anyone at your previous posts able to vouch for you?"

"Sure. I can give you some names." I named the previous five base commanders I'd stayed with. Any would tell him that I'd earned the right to call myself a slayer. It was a term I carried with pride and had inked into a bicep.

"Fine. If what you tell me is backed up by them, then you're on the team."

He turned away and made a notation on his electronic pad before turning back to us. He picked out those that obviously met his needs, and the others slouched, accepting their dismissal with ill grace.

"I want you to meet back here at 0700 tomorrow. You'll need to prepare to be on the road for a minimum of seven to ten days to complete this mission. I'll update you in the morning on the details. You're dismissed."

The six of us who'd been successful looked at each other. This wasn't like any team prep I'd ever attended, and judging by the surprised looks on their faces, they were unused to this type of organization too.

I scratched my chin, the stubble catching on my fingers. "Sir, can you tell us—"

"Not now, Leroy. Tomorrow. 0700."

Dismissed, we filed out of the office.

I waited until the door was closed then turned and addressed the others. "I've never—" The single woman of the group shook her head. "Not here. Not now. Meet in the mess hall at 1500 hours, and we'll discuss it then."

The others grunted assent, and I wondered at this woman who exuded leadership so easily for a young person.

Then she turned and left us there.

I was also intrigued, perplexed that no one voiced any dissent. Strong women. I smiled.

They either made the team work or were quickly replaced.

With that I turned and headed to the bunkroom I'd been assigned.

Julia

I wondered who he was. Where he had come from.

He had that angry 'I just want to kill someone' look about him. I'd seen it dozens of times. I'd also seen the result that came with the loss of care and attention when someone was set on killing. Every time it had come at the cost of someone else's life.

The need to question the commander rose, but I swallowed it, intent on learning more about this person before I spoke. So as the others trailed Leroy to his assigned bunkroom, I watched and waited from the corner where I hid.

He didn't speak. There was no acknowledgement that he knew anyone was there, and that sent a chill tickling my spine uncomfortably. Over the last few months, I'd come to rely on those senses. They'd kept me alive in a lot of bad situations.

I made up my mind, stepped out from where I hid, and followed the unknown man to room 205.

He stopped then turned to me. "What?" One single, tersely spoken word.

I knew all the others in this new team. They were all good fighters, but none of them had leadership potential. I sighed. "Before we head out with you, we need to know who you are. Your history. The motivation for stopping here at Camp Queanbeyan."

He cocked his head and stared at me.

I think it was supposed to make me cower. There wasn't much anymore that did though. Not after all I'd seen, done, and been through.

"Why?"

"Because if you join us, our lives could very well be in your hands. We'll meet you in the mess hall at 1500 to talk. Be there or expect us to block your membership of the team with the commander."

On that note, I spun and strode away. He was watching me though; I felt it. The heat at the back of my neck. *Don't turn around.*

I headed for Commander Dean's office. I had questions and the seniority to demand answers. Two sharp raps and the door opened.

The commander peered around the corner of it. "You took longer than I expected." The door slid open wider, and I pushed inside.

"Sir, I have some concerns—"

"I thought you might." He frowned. "I've made some calls. He's good. Very good. A qualified sharpshooter and an asset to your team."

Sharpshooter. We didn't have one anymore, not since Jen... I shied away from the thought. Thinking about Jen didn't help the situation.

"He might be the best shot in the world, but he has attitudinal issues." I wasn't going to pussyfoot around. Right now I needed to state my case and get his decision.

The commander stared at me. "We can't afford to be choosy these days. If we did, none of us would make the cut."

The gentleness of his words couldn't disguise the sting of truth. Those words didn't assuage the pit that opened in my belly. I had seniority, sure, but I also had responsibilities. A lot of my team members had families in the secure zone. They had kids and partners. Someone waiting for them. I took their concerns and lives seriously.

"You want me to place the lives of my team in his hands." My lips firmed, while I balled my hands into fists.

"Yes and no. I want you to be sure before you head out. I want you to lead the team and complete the extraction. It's imperative we get our operative back here in one piece."

I frowned over his word choice. "Operative?"

The commander slumped into his chair, his fingers tunneling through his salt-and-pepper hair. "Yeah, about that..."

He waved to the seat before the desk, and I dropped into it, staring at the man I thought had told me everything. After all, wasn't I the best team leader and tactician here?

"This mission is sensitive."

I considered his words. "So why didn't you come to me to pick a team?"

He winced, and I leaned forward.

"Because of Allan."

That was akin to a fist in the stomach. Allan. My stepfather and number one weasel. The bastard worked for the government and was too busy to go home to save my mother and sister. Acid ate at my gut. "Allan?"

"Yeah. He's been—"

"No." Dammit, I didn't want to know what happened to him. After all, he'd gone off and left my mother and sister to the tender mercies of...

"J, I need you on this."

I wrenched myself out of the chair and stalked to the door. "I don't want—"

"Dammit, Julia. There's more to this than meets the eye, and trust me, you're going to want to be in on this one."

I wrapped my fingers around the door handle.

"I can make it an order if you prefer, Julia. You need to lead this team. For everyone's sake."

I closed my eyes at his tone of command. "Please..."

"Julia?"

I gave a nod. I understood exactly what he was asking. I didn't like it. "I really don't want——"

"Julia. I won't say it again."

"You don't have to, sir. I understand." I did, although I didn't have to like it. I needed to be a professional and shove the knowledge of that no-good creep from my mind. I had a team, and they relied on me.

"Good."

Leroy
1500

The woman the others called J was sitting at the table. In between terse answers to her team, she shot me hostile looks, and the rest of those assembled were sharing unsettled glances between themselves. If their actions were anything to go by, this wasn't the norm. She was the clearly established leader here and the one I needed to work with; otherwise it would be impossible to fulfill the role I'd agreed to play.

If she couldn't accept me, I'd need to move on, but I needed to replenish my stocks, which had become perilously low. It was an unwritten rule that in order to request provisions, you had to offer some kind of service, and this was the kind of thing I was best at. Killing and vermin eradication.

I wriggled my butt in the vinyl booth, holding the mug between my hands. Before the virus this had been a major hospital for the region, and the existing resources had been repurposed.

"So, Leroy. What's your story?"

I didn't pretend to misunderstand her. I placed the mug on the scarred tabletop. "It's true that I'm itinerant. I don't like to stay in any one place too long. I'd rather do a month or two then move along."

The smile she shot at me didn't warm the ice in her gaze. "So you don't stay anywhere long enough to fit in. Yet I've been informed you're an ace sharpshooter with wicked skills and now you're to join our team."

Ahh, we were getting to the crux of the matter. She didn't want me to make a bad decision that would affect any of the members of the group. "Look. I've seen enough blood and zombies to fill a sea. I'm not looking to short-change anyone. I'm good at what I do and don't intend to see anyone in the group left behind."

"But when the chips are down—"

I'd heard this argument before too. "I don't leave people behind. If necessary, I ensure they won't reanimate."

Now the others at the table shifted uncomfortably.

The man nearest me cleared his throat. "You've done that before?"

"Yeah. A time or two." At the general sound of concern, I settled on a conciliatory tone.

"I don't know anything about you." I pointed at the unknown woman. "I might have concerns of my own." I didn't, but she exuded such an air of disapproval that the words just slipped out.

"What?" The woman—J—surged up, her face a mask of anger.

This wasn't going well. I grunted, "Look, I don't know your name, how many zombies you've faced, or how long you've led this team. I don't know anything about you, yet you question me like I'm some kind of 'innocent'." Yeah, I couldn't resist the air quotes, and she loosed a strangled noise that I knew meant I'd jerked her chain, just a little. "You want to know about me? Well, turnabout's fair play."

The fury in her eyes flashed to a hot, heated emotion, which if I'd had to name it was in the region of *hatred*. Waves of rage licked at me, rolling off her like a tangible, scorching tsunami.

"Fine. The team calls me J. I've been leading them for just under a year, and yes, I've killed a lot of zombies. I couldn't count them."

"Great, J. Would you introduce me to the rest of your team?" I kept my voice mild. I really didn't want to needle her further, and clearly, she needed time to back down off the flare of temper she'd been surfing.

"This is Reg. He's married with two surviving children." She patted the hand of the man who'd held her back. "Dove here was a priest, and he's an awesome lookout and medic."

Dove was the close-cropped, dark-haired guy sitting closest to her. I wondered briefly about his name but knew now wasn't the time to ask.

"Van joined us when the train he was on was attacked. He lost his sister, mother, and brother that day." She pointed to the Eurasian guy who nodded. "Jack, who's sitting beside you, was in the army. He's our grunt and a damned fine tactician. He prefers the Steyr rifle."

"It's a hangover from my military days." Jack held out a hand, his pale blue eyes searching my face before giving the first genuine smile I'd received since arriving at Camp Queanbeyan.

"Hi." I gave him a small grin before turning back to J. "What's your story?"

Her lips thinned as tiny, white brackets appeared. "I don't have one." Now she rose. "We meet in the commander's office tomorrow at 0700. I have some details on the mission, but it's best to hear it and the rest of the intel from the commander."

With that the woman stalked from the room while I sat there, wondering how I could feel battered from such a short encounter.

"J has some issues. She lost most of her family in odd circumstances." Dove shrugged and pushed away from the table. "This isn't the way she normally is. She's good at her job, and a fair leader, willing to give everyone a chance. Just give her a go, okay?" He spoke quietly, every word measured, then turned and walked slowly away from the table.

Dove's words made me frown. If she was acting out of the norm, that might not bode well for whatever mission we were about to embark on. Given she had an issue with me at first sight, it was clear I needed to work with the others, to have them accept me.

"Okay, so what do we do while we wait?"

Jack grinned at me. "Do you play poker?"

Chapter 2

Julia

At 0700 I waited outside the commander's door. I'd let my personal anger get in the way of my instincts in front of my team. There was something about Leroy that got under my skin. There was a niggle about him. I couldn't put my finger on it, but I knew I needed to let it wash away for everyone's benefit.

As the team assembled around me, I wondered how I could best get Leroy by himself so I could somehow approach the fact that I'd acted inappropriately. I didn't like having to own up, but if I let it continue, it would fester and affect everyone. If this mission was half as dangerous as any we'd recently undertaken, we'd need our wits about us just to stay alive. I'd already lost far too many good people in the last three months.

As the door opened, we all stood then filed into the small room.

I scanned the room, but the chairs that had sat against the walls were missing. In the center was an old card table. Rickety as they always seemed to be. Rolled up on top was a map. We gathered around it as the commander took position, unfurled the parchment, and weighed it down.

"Your mission is to extract five survivors. One is Allan Anterrum, and two are civilians. Their identity is unknown. The other two have been assisting Anterrum at that location. We received a communiqué that leads us to believe the information they've obtained might assist in halting the virus from mutating further. Personally, and totally off the record, my early information suggested that researchers were working on a vaccine to inoculate the masses."

"Like a child's vaccine?" Van leaned forward hopefully.

"Yes, but even if that were to exist, I don't believe it can undo the damage, Van. It can't be used to save family members who've already succumbed, because we've seen the reality, that these individuals' brains are in a state of decay that cannot be halted. And there is no way to reverse the damage."

The commander cleared his throat, and for a moment a flash of pain lanced me. I too had hoped, for the tiniest of an instant, for a cure. Perhaps then, if I could find my mother and sister—

Van exhaled, the sound echoing in the silence. A look at his face, the bleached white and wide eyes, showed just how totally he was devastated at this pronouncement. I understood that myself, along with the majority of my crew.

"This is a top-priority mission. Any and all resources required will be extended to the team."

I gnawed on my lip. If what the commander was saying was correct, why was this mission being kept secret?

"Sir? Why the secrecy then? Why not throw everything at it?" Leroy asked the question before I could, and I felt a grudging respect for the man.

"This information is volatile. There are those who don't want it made public. To do so would lead to..."

We leaned forward. This mission was taking on the stench of week-old prawns. "Sir?" I prompted the commander in the growing silence.

"People have already been killed to keep this information secret. There were machinations in the government before the outbreak."

I straightened. "What do you mean?" There was clearly more to this mission than Allan and secrets. I needed to know everything before I took my team out there. Knowledge was power, and I'd need every possible drop of intel so we had a fighting chance.

"In the days before everything happened, I got wind of a covert mission, the direction from high up in government. That they'd accessed some new weapon and were using unsuspecting soldiers to spread it. One that did things to people. Turned them into mindless killing machines. By the time I got around to checking things out, it was too late. The illness had spread. From there it went downhill rapidly. We've been working in crisis mode until now. Some months ago, Allan approached me. Told me the little he knew before the outbreak."

The vicious acid in my stomach roiled once more, as it always did when Allan, and what he knew, came to the fore.

"Allan had contacts. He left to investigate, but as you know, that was months ago. We presumed him lost until we received contact two days ago."

Allan had left nearly two months ago from what I understood. I'd been out on a long- range mission when he'd left, and he hadn't exactly left me information, so I had no idea where he'd gone. And why the hell hadn't he been in contact with anyone else long before now?

"Sir? What has he——"

"We agreed he'd head to the government laboratory. The problem is..." He shrugged.

"It's thick with the eternally damned." Dove spoke quietly, summing up the problem as we saw it.

"True. He managed to track down some of the people he needed to talk to at other bases and encampments. He's been searching for others who had information or heard snippets. None of my normal contacts survived the initial wave, which is why it's taken so long." The commander pointed to the location of the lab on the map. "After his arrival, he and those who he collected around him had to hunker down in a building in midtown. There was an attempt to clean out the nest, and while he lost most of his crew, he did find two survivors and some laboratory technicians who had holed up inside the building."

I frowned. Two survivors in a nest of zombies? How could that possibly be?

Opening my mouth to ask just that was met with a stern, "Don't ask me, J, because I don't know about the civilians. What I do know is he's found files and serums on-site. Normally, we'd ask the nearest camp for assistance, but it's critical we don't tip off anyone with a vested interest in keeping this silent at this point. Given the sheer volume of data and samples he's found, he can't get back here on foot by himself. This is where we need him. We've got the resources and some of the staff necessary to hopefully find out what's going on."

It was true. Camp Queanbeyan was based out of the old Canberra General Hospital, but still...

"We need those serums and files. We don't have a working vehicle, but we have an alternative." The commander smiled, and the pit in my stomach yawed wider.

"What?"

"We found an old dray over at the brewery. One of you, surely, would know how to make it work."

Leroy started laughing. "Cute, sir. But we'd need horses."

I'd been ordered to hunt for and retrieve some horses on my last mission. It all made sense now.

"Already under control, right, J?"

I sighed. "Yes, sir. Now I know why you were so insistent."

"Well, the dray will be back here later today. We've made provisions for the horses— constructed a steel cage to protect them, and before you ask, we've constructed wheels for the front so there isn't too much weight and the chance of it falling on the mares. As soon as we can get it attached to the dray, you'll be ready to roll. I have a provisioning team working on your needs. We don't have time to fit a cage to the dray itself, so you'll need to be eyes wide open."

"Sir?" I felt trepidation about this mission as my stomach was curled into tight knots.

"J, we aren't going to get another shot at this. I need my best. That's you and your team."

I swallowed and stepped away. "Yes, sir."

Leroy

The group assembled outside the commander's door.

"So now what?" I asked.

J gave me a look, a stare with a hint of question. "Get whatever you need in a backpack.

I'm going to find the requisition staff and check on med supplies and munitions. I have a feeling we're going to need as much as possible."

She stalked away and left the rest of us standing there. The team, except for Dove and myself, broke away and headed in various directions, likely about to gather their belongings.

I took a moment to size up the quiet, dark-haired man. "You've worked with her for how long?"

Dove shrugged. "A year or so. She's good."

I pinned him with a stare. "You're a priest, right?"

"Yeah. Or I was." He grimaced, clearly discomforted but soldiering on. Whether it was because he felt the need to connect or for absolution I couldn't guess. "I don't kill unless I have to. I'm a medic, radio operator, confessor, and much more besides."

"What about the others?"

He gave me an inscrutable look. "What do you mean?"

"Tell me about their personalities."

"Look, I see others as I find them. That works for me. I would advise you to do the same." He stretched his back then turned, leaving me alone with sure footsteps.

I shook my head. I'd made a rookie mistake.

Heading for the mess, I readjusted my backpack. Where I went, so did it.

No one questioned my attachment to it as I entered the catering area and snatched up a cup which I filled with coffee.

The pack carried all the things that were important to me except the tiny talisman stashed in a pocket. Carefully, I placed the bag beside my feet as I sank to a seat with drink in hand, then lay my rifle across my lap.

I opened the pouch in my pants and reached for the linkages of gold. Hanging at the end of the chain was a ring, the wink of a diamond flashing. For the first time in a long while, I let myself focus on the memento in my hand. It represented the life I'd lost, the one stolen by this plague.

I knew Katrina would never be human again. Couldn't be. The last time I'd seen her the flesh of her face was shredded and gray-green tinged, her hair a grim matting of strands, blood, and other unidentifiable globs. No, she'd never be human again.

I allowed myself to accept that even if I'd been there, I couldn't have saved her. We all knew that once bitten it was only a matter of time. I breathed deeply, the scent of cinnamon and ground beans filling my nostrils.

A hand touched my shoulder. "We've all lost someone close to us. Whoever she was, however important to you, the most integral thing to remember is we are still alive."

J. I clenched my hand into a fist around the necklace and ring, hiding it from view, because it was private. My personal yoke. "Yeah." I stashed them back into the pocket and rose.

"Sit. Finish your coffee, while I drink mine."

J settled herself on the opposite side of the laminate table from me. I stared for a moment or two and subsided back into the squashy padding.

"We got off on the wrong foot, and I need to uh..."

I blinked as she spoke quietly and with conviction, wondering where this was going to go.

"...apologize. I was unprofessional when you turned up."

Straightening in the chair, I thought fast. "Look, I'm here for a while. Long enough to be able to re-provision. I'm not looking for a home, just a way to pay back the camp."

Her lips thinned, and for a moment I was sure I'd said the wrong thing and made it worse, then she gave a curt nod. "Fine then. So we're clear, I'm in need of a sharpshooter for the team. As long as you fulfill that role, everyone will be happy."

Okay. Confusion cascaded at her words. This wasn't quite the outcome I was looking for, but I'd take it, except, what had I expected? Without any answer, I shrugged. "When do we head out?"

"As soon as I finish my coffee."

Slowly, she lifted the cup to her lips, and I watched, fascinated, as her throat moved. I didn't realize I was staring until she cleared her throat.

"Everything okay?" she asked.

With an inaudible sigh I pushed up from the table, feeling down-right foolish. "Yeah."

It had been a long time since I'd felt anything for a woman, and right now? It was hugely inconvenient that my libido found the time to grow some interest.

I slung the pack over my shoulder and gripped the muzzle end of my rifle. "Let's get moving."

***

Julia

On arrival I found the horses had been hitched and their food loaded on the dray in large metal drums, chained in place, along with a drum of fresh water. The team stood around waiting as I clambered up onto the seat, and for a moment, dizziness assailed. I hadn't expected it to be quite so high.

The horses were encased in a mesh and wire cage with what appeared to be stroller wheels. Clearly the powers that be hoped that it would be zombie-proof. I hoped so too.

Dove slid into the seat beside me and took up the reins, after smoothly releasing the brake. "Make yourselves comfortable, friends. We're about to go." He gave a clicking sound and flicked the leads. The horses pranced a little before moving forward with a jerk.

"I didn't know you had knowledge of driving drays."

"I learned while in seminary. We used to run religious camps and had the usual hayride thing happening. Most of us younger brothers learned while the older ones focused on more spiritual interactions with the boys."

I bit my lip, evaluating the sourness of his words. As with the majority of us, he too labored under the immense pressure and sorrow which our new reality shoved us under. There wasn't much to say, so I pressed his hand gently and looked to the road ahead. The weight of my rifle a comfort as we left our metal gated secure zone.

The grating sound of the doors closing behind us ricocheted through my mind, as if urging me on a path I wasn't sure I was ready for. The potholed terrain and wrecks of abandoned cars could hide zombies quite effectively, and now that we'd cleared the gates of the hospital precinct we needed to be on our guard.

"Okay, boys, eyes peeled and look for zombies."

Since the spread of the deadly plague we'd figured out that noise, vibrations, and of course the sight of living humans was enough to work them into a frenzy. The clopping of the horses' hooves and the squeak of their cage we couldn't do anything about, so our best bet was to stay alert.

Within minutes we experienced our first incursion. A group descended, still wearing the shredded remains of school uniforms and doctors' scrubs. Kids were the worst, because even though we knew they'd turned and had no future, the sight of their bodies... I shuddered and shouldered my rifle.

"Remember, they're not kids anymore. They'll bite and turn us, so be on your game."

A rustle beside me alerted me to Dove donning his stole and fishing out bottles of holy oil.

"Dove?" I half-turned in my seat, and the look he shot in my direction ravaged me. Pain had settled on his features, his mouth a flat line of hopelessness, and his eyes had lost the gleam that usually sat there, replaced by dull acceptance.

"Time to give them eternal rest."

It always seemed incongruous to hear Dove offering last rites as we proceeded to complete the death cycle for zombies, but he did that now, his voice somber and determined over the *phut* sound of bullets entering flesh.

I listened to the cadence of "May the Lord who frees you from sin save you and raise you up," with each shot, waiting for the splash of black-red, congealing blood and the thud of the body dropping to the pitted asphalt. The smell, as always, overpowered my senses.

Then there was silence.

I always found it eerie after a skirmish. No birdsong, no moans or shuffles. Instead, this time the horses gave a snuffle, and after a quick rustle, Dove took up the reins again.

"You handled that well." Leroy's words over my shoulder reminded me that he hadn't been with us long enough to be comfortable with how we worked.

As I opened my mouth to reply, I heard a new sound. A growl, dog-like and loud.

"We should get out of here now." Dove spoke loudly and gee'd the horses up, so that the dray rumbled and clattered faster than before.

"Shit!" Ahead of us were three large dogs. The red glow of their eyes and the matted, greasy fur told me they'd been bitten at some time. Zombified dogs had become more of a concern lately.

"My turn. Shove over a little, J."

Leroy shuffled so he leaned on the seat between Dove and myself, the long muzzle of his rifle steady, amazing though it seemed as we shuttled forward. One quick ping and the first dog dropped. It propelled the others forward. I heard a mutter then another ping saw the second dog drop. It wouldn't be enough though, because the third was running.

I shouldered my rifle, sighted, and squeezed the trigger, waiting, exhaling slightly and hoping. A splash showed on the pelt, and the impact slowed it but didn't stop the creature.

My heart thudded rapidly against my ribs.

Another ping and it fell to the ground, and I inhaled deeply.

"That was close. Is this a new thing?" Leroy's question pulled me from my momentary distraction.

"We're seeing more of it now, as the zombies are searching for prey and the dogs are starving. They're taking more chances, and of course..." Dove didn't finish the sentence, but I knew Leroy understood the unspoken words.

Where the zombies and dogs converged, it was only a matter of time until they too were bitten and turned. Zombie dogs were a whole lot more frightening, because they were hunting machines with speed and savagely sharp nails and teeth.

Leroy pulled back and settled against the raised bench. "I haven't encountered this phenomenon before."

I wondered what he'd seen, as he'd dealt with them quickly and efficiently. He hadn't seemed disturbed at dealing with the zombie children, and that gave me a moment of disquiet.

Leroy

The thud and clatter of hooves and metal wheels lulled me, so I lay back, watching behind us for signs of—well, not exactly life, but movement. I'd caught the flash of awareness in J's eyes as I'd euthanized the dogs, and I knew my ability to do the same to the children had surprised her. Maybe even disturbed her on some level. I didn't like it, found it hard, but knew the realities. No one probably knew them more than I did.

She didn't know about my background, and I guessed that discussion point would rise at some stage. She'd want to know who and what I was, just as much as I wanted to forget.

We traveled for an hour or two with no other incursions, while the sun rose in the sky. Around midday, we found an open area. It was flat and easy to defend while affording clear sight all around for some distance. We removed the cage from around the horses to allow them to drink but stayed on alert.

The rest was welcome, but the group remained subdued. I wondered if that was normal after a brief battle, or if it was the result of the group being made up of previous-life civilians. The sun beat down, the grass waved back and forth, and for a short time I could forget that the world was no longer the civilized lifestyle I'd lived before.

"Leroy? What did you do before this?" J dropped down beside me, the grass crunching and her voice soft.

"I was a soldier." That didn't really explain what I'd been, but the truth was unpalatable.

Something I'd hidden for a long time.

"Oh. Were you based here? On secondment?"

J didn't take the hint, and I wanted to tell her to stop asking, but what benefit would that be to me? "No." I wondered if changing the subject would re-direct her attention. "So what does J stand for?"

"Julia. My name is Julia, but in the middle of firefights it's inconvenient, so I became J." She shrugged, her mane of red-gold hair glinting and playing around her shoulders.

"Did you grow up in Canberra?"

She gave a harsh laugh. "No. I was here because my stepfather was placed here, and my mother and little sister came with him. I was here on holidays when everything happened. So I stayed in the hopes that..." Now her words died away, and I understood.

"I'm sorry. Did they suffer?"

When she turned away, her shoulders shook slightly. Dammit, I'd made the tough woman cry.

"I'm sorry, J. I didn't mean to remind you."

"No. You've a right to ask. I don't know." Her arms moved, and I guessed she was swiping away the tears that thickened her voice. "Allan said he tried to get to them. I was out sight-seeing. I'd gotten a lift with him because Abby was at school and Mum wanted to get her hair done. I haven't seen them since that morning."

I sighed. I'd been in the heart of this zombie mess, and a fat blob of emotion was attacking me, leaving me feeling a confusing mix of guilt and softness. Neither of which I wanted to experience. Emotions weren't important anymore. At least not to me.

J pushed up from the ground without looking back at me, and for the first time, I made out the slender curves of the woman, a flash of pale pink skin drawing my eye.

"We should hitch up and move out," she said. "We need to make the airport tonight."

"J..." I reached out, and she turned back, just enough that I could see the shimmer of tears in her eyes. "You need to know—"

"No, Leroy. I don't need to know what happened to them. I wish I would find them alive, but realistically..."

She'd assumed something totally different to what I'd been about to say. The splash of acid that burned my throat at how she'd react if I told her what I'd done and been stopped any further words from emerging.

It was foolish and pathetic, but I grabbed the easy way out with both hands.

Pushing away from the ground, I brushed the grass from the seat of my pants and started heading for the dray. "I'll get Dove's assistance to hitch the horses back up."

J didn't respond, just turned her back and looked out over the wilderness behind us.

Julia

Approaching the heart of what had been Canberra was disquieting.

I trudged one weary foot in front of the other. "How are the horses holding up?"

"Better now that most of the weight is off the dray." Dove spoke quietly.

We'd pulled up at the old War Memorial last night and he'd declared the horses were finding the weight hard. As a group we'd decided that walking would be better to help them make it to the end of the mission.

We'd be traveling for two and a half days, and I had to be honest, the commander had been right. Skirting the main areas of town had meant only smaller packs of zombies. The center of Canberra was clearly visible as it had been for a fair chunk of yesterday.

"I wonder how many zombies are in Parliament House?" Van's voice echoed with mirth. A laugh rippled among the group.

"They were zombies before the plague." Jack snickered.

"You could be on to something." I flicked another look in the direction of the center.

Memories of my citizenship education classes reminded me that Canberra hadn't been settled over a period of time, rather a town built around Lake Burley Griffin with the intention of becoming the heart of Australia.

I glanced ahead and contemplated what I could see. Anzac Avenue was exposed. My stomach was tied in knots. In the distance lay Parkes Way. The back of my neck itched, and I gripped my rifle tightly. The closer we came to what had been a heavily populated area, the deeper the danger. I felt it keenly.

"Hey, J? What's that blob ahead?" Dove called out to me, the horses and dray in the center of the team while I'd taken the right flank.

I squinted, looking into the distance. "I don't know." My senses screamed it was something I didn't want to know, and dread filled me as the blob moved apart, separating into smaller moving parts. "Incoming!"

We moved like a well-oiled machine, tightening the pack so we flanked the dray and horses as we moved forward. Leroy vaulted onto the back of the dray, a statue exuding confidence as he shouldered his rifle.

Five... Six... Dammit, ten shambling zombies were heading in our direction. I wasn't happy to be found here on the outskirts of the town. We could beat these ones, but my greater concern was how much noise we were about to make becoming an invitation to more. There were plenty enough heading toward us, as if we were a large magnet. More could potentially swamp us.

"Pull up and let them come to us."

Dove gave me a look that clearly said 'you're crazy', his eyes wide as he stared at me, but he hauled the horses to a stop.

"If we engage them here, the noise won't carry so far," I explained. "We don't want to attract any more than we have to deal with."

"That's it, just a little closer." The whisper of Leroy's words impinged.

I sighted the zombies and waited, inhaling lightly.

The tiny thud and *oomph* from the man beside me, together with the toppling of the zombie, told me the bullet had found its mark. The sound of the reload echoed as I checked my aim and squeezed the trigger. The kickback jerked, the wood of the barrel digging into my shoulder.

Another dropped. The others took aim and fired while Dove intoned the world of the last rites again, but this time he held the reins tightly. The sound must have been startling to the horses as they shuffled a little.

Another *phut* beside me, and finally, the puffs of smoke that had filled the air cleared. One lone zombie dragged itself in our direction. Van cursed and lowered his rifle.

"Hold your ground, Van."

Surprisingly, he didn't listen. Instead, he mumbled something and strode forward, each step faster than the last.

Jack hurried, his hand outstretched as if to grab him, but Van shrugged him off.

I knew what this meant. It happened sometimes. The constant death and slaughter became too much for a person to handle. He'd snapped.

Jack grabbed for him again, meaty fingers grabbing Van's shoulder. "Stop, man!"

He tugged the Eurasian man toward him, and I caught a glimpse of the pain on Van's face.

"It's not them," Jack said.

The wail of zombies rent the air, and I cursed and turned to the others. "Get on the dray now!"

I had a sudden sensation of doom. The clench of my stomach and the prickling feeling increased. We were out in the open, still some distance from our destination, and one of my team was emotionally compromised. It spelled disaster.

"Dove? Get us out of here now," I ordered.

He did, clicking at the horses and sending them forward. He stopped momentarily beside the men and Jack shoved Van onto the back.

I touched Van's shoulder. "Give me your rifle."

He stared at me, a blank expression on his face. I grabbed the rifle, and Van dissolved, hunched into himself.

Right now there wasn't time to evaluate his condition. His scream had sounded loudly, and the sound of moans and growls filled the air. My mouth dried.

The horses moved as quickly as possible while the men, rifles ready for action, did what they had to. The violence leaving Van rolling on the wooden platform.

If I wasn't so worried, I might have made a comment that it seemed somewhat surreal. Weird and mind-numbing almost. So many forms came at us.

"Can we go faster?" I asked.

Dove's expression shut me up. Clearly that wasn't a useful question. So I joined the work of the others, the constant thuds and *phuts* of firing weapons melding with the clop of the hooves and the squeak of wheels.

Ahead lay the shimmering waters of Lake Burley Griffin and beyond that the decaying remains of the impressive parkway. This was the most dangerous part of our journey. Once we entered the parkway, we were in what had been a densely populated area. Full of zombies.

I licked my dry lips as I scanned the horizon.

Leroy

As fast as we aimed and shot, another one or two zombies appeared. This was just the tip though. Once we were on the approach to the laboratory, there would be more. Lots more. They congregated in areas that had been busy, because that's where they'd find food.

"We need to get off this road." The clip of my G2A was empty, and I was struggling to find another filled clip in my pocket.

"No. This puts us in the right area to approach the lab. Next door is an abandoned hotel, which has an underground parking area. So long as it's clear, it's a defensible place to leave the horses and Van. Probably Jack too."

I glanced in J's direction and noticed her biting her lip. Yeah, Van's breakdown was a massive problem for the team. Hopefully he could pull it together enough to hang on.

We hit the end of the motorway and turned onto the road beside the water. It wasn't going to be far, but we'd have to outrun and outthink the zombies.

"We need to get into the car park?" I asked.

"Yeah."

My mind whirled. "And you intend to do that, how?"

"I haven't worked that out yet." Julia's voice was stiff, and I understood she felt threatened by my questioning.

Shit! "So what, we'll just stroll up and see if there's any zombies and ride the dray in?"

"Dammit, Leroy—"

"Stop it you two." Dove's voice cut through our argument. "J, I see what Leroy is saying. We need a distraction so we can check the environment out."

Julia subsided, the woman sighing and pulling at her hair as she thought. Funny how I suddenly thought of her as a woman, not just a fellow soldier. The sensation was wholly unwelcomed.

With so much weight on the dray, the horses were struggling. They panted, and their sides lathered with a white foam. "We need to get off this, otherwise we won't get there."

Dove glanced at me. "You know a little about horses?"

"Not much, but enough to know that the longer we keep them under this kind of load, the sooner they'll break down."

Dove grunted.

"I say Jack, Reg, and I take up the rear. We're quick and armed. You, Van, and Dove go ahead. We'll meet up with you at the entrance to the hotel... What did you call it?"

"The Neapolitan," Dove answered, and I glanced at him again. "I was based here for several years before the plague. I officiated at weddings and was a guest at the hotel on several occasions. The entrance to the car park is up the center. There are only a few places where we could be ambushed, so it's highly defendable. That's assuming there arc no zombies inside the car park itself."

"Good then. Van? Are you up to helping Dove and J?"

The wild look he gave me left me more uncertain than I'd been in the past, but hell, I needed him, if not on his game, at least useful right now. I'd have to take a chance.

"Ye... Yeah. I think so."

I caught the eyes of Jack and Reg, then we slipped down the back of the dray to the asphalt.

Dropping to my knees, the sting of stones reminded me that we needed to move. "Come on!"

The three of us took up defensive positions at the back of the cart, holding onto our guns as we made our way up the road.

We walked, the sun beating down on us as we trudged, alert and aware until we reached the final approach.

"Dove? We'll go ahead and clear the entrance. Van? Stay alert. J?" I looked at her and realized I didn't quite know what to say. Everything would sound inane because I was suddenly aware that she, most of all, had wormed her way into the area I'd kept shut off from everyone around me. "Stay safe."

Without thinking any further, we peeled off and started running, knowing that we might never meet again.

Chapter 3

Julia

As we rumbled around the corner, I gripped my rifle tight, senses alert, thankful that until now we'd seen no zombies.

It felt different coming into Canberra proper after all this time. The emptiness, abandoned vehicles, and broken glass made it feel like an alien world.

The whole time I looked around, billowing materials fluttering in the breeze through smashed windows and a layer of dust covering everything we passed.

We'd seen more than one skeleton, a sobering reminder that we were no longer the alpha predator. No, we were fodder for those mindless creatures that now preyed on us.

The building loomed ahead, and we rolled around the corner. No zombies. I breathed deeply for the first time since half my team had left. Now, if only they were there waiting.

"Dove, let's slow down a bit, just in case they haven't cleared the area—"

Small arms fire started, and I swallowed. Did that mean the team had made it? Or was it a wild attempt to let us know that the mission was a failure?

I squinted into the gloom.

"There!" Dove gestured to an opening,

Jack was waving both arms, indicating we should move. The urgency had my blood humming.

"Where are the others?" I scanned the area but didn't see Reg or Leroy. Reg had been with me since the beginning, but Leroy? I really didn't want to accept that he fascinated me, or that losing him now would wound me.

I bit down on my lip as we rumbled into the parking area. The empty area surprised me. I'd been sure that it couldn't possibly be empty.

"They're clearing the building. We found a few starving zombs, but Jack and Leroy were adamant that we needed to check everywhere in the building then secure this zone."

"Oh. Good, then we should unhitch the horses. Dove?"

"We need to close the gates first and secure them." Dove threw me the chain and lock, and I moved quickly, the weight and noise settling my nerves.

He'd already dropped to the ground when I rejoined him. Dove was so soft and gentle with the mares. I forgot that so often because he was one of the team. The smile he gave me, his eyes crinkling at the corners, had me smiling in return.

"How about you set up the stove and organize a coffee while I get busy here?" He pulled the box of equipment from the dray and placed it on the ground beside me.

"Uh, sure."

He set to work as I unpacked the small propane burner, pot, bottle of water, and other necessities, including the premade food we'd packed.

A *whir* started up and lights blazed. I sucked in my breath as Reg and Leroy entered the underground area from the access door. We rolled the already unloaded drums in front of the door. It would do until we could find keys to lock the door properly.

"Coffee? Excellent." Reg headed in my direction while Leroy

headed for Dove, assisting in removing the cage and unhooking the horses.

I watched Leroy and Dove covertly. Two very different men, yet both of them strong and capable in their own way.

When they came over, after hobbling the horses and setting out water and food, they crouched beside me, gratefully accepting the drinks.

"Now, we're here and the building is just across the way. How are we going to manage this?" Dove's quiet tone settled me.

"I'm thinking we should leave Van and Reg here to finish setting up an overnight camp, while the other four of us make our way over to the lab building. It's just across the way, but you know how it is, there's many a slip and all that."

Leroy nodded. "I think that's best. Where in the lab will we find them?"

Dove held up the tiny radio. "We came to an agreement months ago that we use one channel exclusively. I'd be surprised if they don't have access to a unit. Once we're ready, we should call them and find out exactly where we meet them."

"Cool. Drink up then, so we can get moving." Now that we were close nervous energy flooded my system. "Reg, I need you to finish getting this place ready and take care of Van."

Reg simply nodded at the direction.

"The generator is working, so I'm thinking we should drag some bedding down here, because I doubt we'll be leaving here today," Leroy said.

Those words bothered me, immensely. "Why?"

"Because we're supposed to gather the files and vials, plus a couple of civilians. I doubt we'll get out of here with everything before dark, so we should start to organize ourselves to bunk down here tonight."

Certainly I'd slept in worse conditions before, but something about this felt off. My mind crawled with scenarios of what could go wrong and being cornered, yet out there would be worse.

"Once we start to prepare food we might as well put out a huge beacon to the zombies." My words sounded weak, even to myself.

Dove covered my hand. "We've been in tighter corners before, and tonight, we're in a defensible position. Besides, we can hide the light easily, with bedding from the hotel rooms above."

They were right, but I felt that we were exposed with so many damned unknowns.

I finished my coffee, wiped out my cup, and stowed it back in the box. "Right, let's get moving then."

Dove collected his radio and bag while the others caught up their rifles, and as one, we moved to the door leading to the heart of the hotel.

Leroy

We moved together, a fluid group, while Dove spoke quietly into the radio. I stuck close to J, my attention split between her and the need to be aware of any incoming attacks. I'd already scouted out the back door to the hotel and opened it just a crack, thankful the door didn't squeak. The coast looked clear, so I crooked my finger, indicating they should follow.

We stopped at the edge of the building, peering around corners. No zombies that I could see. As one we crossed the street, moving rapidly. We needed to get around the street corner and up the stairs. It should be clear, but you couldn't be sure.

We'd almost reached the corner when Dove held up a hand and waved to the earpiece he was using with the handset. "Wait!" His word was barely whispered. "There's another entry, halfway down the road. They're going to open it and let us in. There's zombs in the building, but this is the secured, safe entrance."

I frowned at his words. If it was secured, there had to be power, otherwise how were they getting in and out? A question for later.

I glanced at the side of the building, looking for the door. I spied it just as it opened, and we hurried in its direction. Just as we reached the edge of the building, I heard the sound I dreaded. A low, dirge-like moan. "Zombies on the way. Speed up."

As one, we now sprinted, using every ounce of energy to get us to the entry. We'd nearly made it to the steps when J tripped. She cried out, and the zombies stopped, realigned themselves, and I started to sweat.

"Hang on. Dove, take my stuff." I shoved my rifle into his hands and headed back to where J was splayed on the ground, gripping her ankle while silent tears rolled down her cheeks.

"Hurry!" someone called to us as I reached down and scooped the woman up.

"My stuff." She spoke with a snuffle, but Jack was there, already collecting it.

Now laden with the injured woman and her pack, we hurried, not quite a run but as fast as we could manage. The zombies were closing in as we made it to the steps. We scampered down and through the door before they could catch up to us.

Inside, the lights blared, and I sucked in my breath, thankful we'd made it this far. "That was too close," Jack muttered, and I had to agree.

The man on the door slammed it shut after we cleared the doorway. "Through here."

"Allan?" J's voice was thready and weak as she turned in my arms.

"Yeah. Bring Julia this way." He led us down a stairway and past a glass door with a card entry. "Julia, prepare yourself."

She squirmed in my arms as we pushed past the jamb. "What are you talking about?"

"I found your mother and sister. Julia, they're here."

"What? You found my zombie mother and sister and brought them here? Why? Why would you do that? Don't you have—"

"Allan? Is that Julia, darling?"

Julia stilled in my arms, and I'm not sure what I felt...

"Mum?" She barely spoke; in fact, I detected a whisper of disbelief.

"Darling? What happened to you?" A woman in her late forties, her clothes hanging on a spare frame, rushed over and grabbed J, patting her face and hair, anything she could get her hands on.

For a moment, I wanted to rip J away and hug her close so I could check and make sure she was indeed fine. A thoroughly unnerving reaction.

"Hang on. Let's just find somewhere to put her so Dove can check her leg." I scttled J into the padding of the seat inside the room.

A girl about twelve came barreling out of the room. "Mum?"

"Look, it's Julia, Ab. We're all back together again."

Julia

My mother. Abby. How could this be? Perhaps the fall had actually been worse than I thought and I banged my head? This had to be some coma-driven fantasy. *Right?*

"Mum?" The word slipped from my mouth, and I reached out, fingers curling then tugging back before touching. If this was a dream, then they were likely zombies.

I curled in on myself, ready to propel myself forward and away, but she grasped me. I felt the heat of her body, the suppleness of her skin. No groan or moan emitted, and deep inside my chest, the frozen section warmed.

"Yes, darling. Now we need this lovely young man to check you out." My mum was beaming at Dove like he was some angel of mercy. And as soon as she spoke the pain radiated from my leg.

"Come on, J. Let me see what's happening and fix you up." Dove spoke quietly, in that reassuring way I'd heard countless times before. The softly sexy voice married with his wicked hardness. It made him... I stopped my thoughts before they got out of hand. After all, Dove was a priest!

"Uh, it's my leg."

He smiled, the corner of his mouth ticking up while the lines at the edges of his eyes crinkled deeply. The blue of his irises mesmerized me.

Leroy cleared his throat. "Sir? You must be Allan Anterrum? We were sent here to collect you, the two civilians, your assistants, and the files?"

"Yes. Myself, my wife and daughter, and two scientists. They've been living here since the plague outbreak."

I heard Leroy—I needed to really find out if that was his first or last name—and Allan talking, at least I listened until Dove moved my leg, pulled my trouser leg up, and started his inspection of the injury. Then a lance of pain shot through every nerve, and I arched my back, an involuntary reaction to the stimulus.

"Oh God! Dove! What are you doing to me?"

"It's okay, J. It looks like a severe sprain rather than a break. So it could be worse. We can strap it up to get you back to our transportation. Then the doctors back at camp can take a look at it."

"Dammit, Dove, you're wasted as a priest."

He stilled at my muttered words, and I closed my eyes. What a grossly stupid thing to say!

"I wasn't a Catholic priest, you know. I can still marry. Or I would if..." He sounded disgusted by my words.

I gaped at him, then shook my head. I guessed I must have glowed like the proverbial light bulb, if the heat radiating from my neck and chest were anything to go by.

"Dove, I'm sorry. I shouldn't have—"

"Yeah, well, don't worry." The brush-off made me feel guilty and small, while my chest tightened under an impossible pressure.

I wanted to apologize, but before I could say any more, Allan was there. "How are you, Julia?"

"I'm fine. Or I will be. Dove thinks it's a sprain, so I'll recover." My heart beat rapidly as I waited for Allan to say something, anything, that would let on to my mother how I'd treated him since losing her. I'd spoken harshly on more than one occasion, accusing him of being uncaring and unconcerned about her loss and Abby's.

"I'm glad." He slid a hand over the top of my head, and I closed my eyes.

"Allan, I'm—"

"Shhh. It's okay. I understand, trust me."

Guilt spread through me, but before I could say anything more, he turned away.

"How soon can we get moving, and what transportation do you have?" he asked.

Leroy strode forward, glancing only quickly in my direction. "Sir, we can be on the way in the morning. We have to make the airport—there's a secure base there now—and we have two horses and a dray. Depending on the amount of data and equipment, plus the civilians, it's going to be a slow journey, and one I don't recommend in the dark."

It felt odd not to be making the decisions, but Leroy slipped into the role of team leader as if it were a second skin. At that moment, I decided I needed to discover more about his history.

"So where is the cart? And when do you intend to load up?" Allan settled in the old computer chair he'd tugged away from the console.

"It's in the car park at the Neapolitan Hotel. Depending on how much there is, we can load up now, bunk down there for the night, and head out as early as first light."

Allan seemed to consider Leroy's answer then frowned. "I'll show you and the rest of the team what we have, then you can work out how to ferry it all. There are a couple of trolleys, so they might help."

Jack, Leroy, and Dove trailed after Allan while Mum and Abby gathered close.

"We didn't think you'd survived. Mum said..." Abby broke off and started to cry, her hand over her face.

"How did you?" I levered up off the couch where Dove had carried out his assessment.

"When it happened, I saw them falling and turning. It was awful, you know? I ran as fast as I could to the house. Mum hadn't left for the hairdresser yet, so we holed up in the house for a day or two. When the food ran out and the power failed, Mum got on the landline while it was still working. Mr. Coventry at the post office said he heard there was a safe place at the police station, so we went there. They turned it into a camp until Dad came and found us. We'd given up hope."

Abby's shoulders shook, and I reached over and tugged her close. I too understood giving up hope.

"When Allan brought us here, he said he knew where you were. That you were safe the last time he'd seen you, but that it had been some weeks. We've been here about four weeks." Mum looked at me, and I felt sure she knew how I'd acted toward my stepfather.

"Mum, I said and did—"

"It's okay, Julia. We've all done things we've regretted. The important thing is we have time to fix these things and make them right. Now, Allan says that Camp Queanbeyan has all sorts of facilities, and did you say you had horses? I haven't seen any in so long!" She waved her hands, just like she always had when she got excited.

"Yeah. We'll be traveling on a dray, just like in the olden days." I tried to inject as much mirth as possible into my voice, in the hopes of lightening the atmosphere, though I still felt the guilt of my actions pressing down on me.

Leroy

There were indeed boxes of files and serums, and God knew what else, but the two scientists were quick to inform me that most of the information had been carefully backed up onto thumb drives since the plague had hit.

"So we need these three boxes of drives and two of serums? Anything else?" I asked.

"The paper files are important, but we've managed to get it down to four archive boxes and the backup computers here." The older scientist, probably in his fifties, given the salt-and- pepper that liberally sprinkled his formerly dark hair, indicated to a pile of five laptops, each carefully packed in padded backpacks.

"All right then. You said there was a trolley?"

I glanced at Allan Anterrum. I don't know what I expected

really. I knew he was J's stepfather, but I guess I thought there'd be something in common in their looks. He didn't resemble Julia at all though. Where he was a receding blond, Julia had a hot shimmering red head of hair. He was spare-framed whereas Julia had curves, not a lot, but enough to hold and enjoy. His face echoed the years of hardship we'd all lived through, where Julia's was sun-kissed and smooth.

Julia looked more like her mother, and Abby, her little sister, was similar except with her father's blue-gray eyes. I preferred Julia's bright green, and the way she smiled made the sun and moon bask in her reflection.

"Leroy? Is everything okay?"

I shook myself at Allan's query. *Daydreaming. Urgh!*

"Fine. We need to pack everything up. Make sure anything we need is easily at hand, because once we leave, coming back will be almost an impossibility. Do either of you know how to shoot a rifle?" I glanced at the two scientists.

The older man shook his head.

The woman, in her early thirties, smiled. "I can. I grew up on a farm, so I learned young."

"Can you handle this one?" I handed her Julia's bolt action 33.

She took it gingerly and ensured the bolt was disengaged. She glanced down, checking to make sure there was no bullet in the action, and shrugged. "Sure. It's pretty simple." She slung it over her shoulder.

"We'd best be quick, so we can get across the way and into the building before night falls. By the way, I'm Leroy." I held out my hand and she clasped it.

"Veronica. This is Dave, and you already met Allan."

I waved the others forward. "Dove and Jack. We've also got Ju —" I stopped myself, then breathed deeply. "J. She's sprained her ankle, and according to Dove, she'll require assistance to get back to the garage."

"Fine then. Maybe if we get Abby and Helen to push the trolleys, leaving Dave and Allan free to help J, the three of us can protect the group. We can each carry a laptop, because they'll swing over our shoulders without getting in the way." Veronica spoke briskly and started packing up the boxes as she spoke. I admired her planning skills.

Once we were ready, I organized the group, after a glance at J. Her white face and a quick nod of her head when I suggested that perhaps it might be best if she let us take the lead, did little to disquiet my concern.

So, with Helen pushing a trolley, and Dave and Allan bolstering J while the younger sister pushed the other trolley at the center of the group, we made for the door. We'd lashed the boxes to the trolley, so if we needed to move quickly, they wouldn't fall and have to be abandoned. Jack led the way with a laptop bag hung over his back, Dove slightly left and similarly loaded, while I took up the right rear. My bag swung annoyingly, but we needed all the information we had on hand. It wasn't perfect, but the best we could do under the circumstances.

"Ready to move?" I cast an eye over the group.

"Just a minute," the young woman, Veronica, toting the rifle stopped us. "I'm going to rig an alarm and the lighting so it attracts the zombies to the front of the building. That way, we should be able to get out without being accosted."

I had to admit to finding her lack of fear both refreshing and slightly disturbing at the same time.

Veronica tugged on a cover, revealing a power board, lights blinking on and off. A few quick input taps seemed to do the trick as she shut the metal door with a slam. "We've got maybe five minutes until it attracts them. Wait by the door and keep an eye out."

Jack cracked the door open while everyone else waited, quiet and ready to move at any second. Time passed slowly. It felt like hours yet must have been a matter of minutes, then Jack nodded and I gave the unspoken 'move out' gesture with my hand.

We stayed together, moving up the stairs, Julia limping in the middle of the group, and I knew it must have been intolerably painful, yet she didn't so much as squeak.

We stopped, and once more took a precious second, searching for anything untoward.

Danger lurked everywhere, and caution had kept all of us alive for a long time.

Satisfied, we started across the road. It wasn't wide, but it was dotted with abandoned dumpsters. We walked quickly without a word when the growl started.

"Shit. Dogs." The words slipped from Julia's lips as she looked around wildly. "Keep moving." I kept my voice as low and as calm as I could. We didn't want to act scared, as whatever kind they were, it was clear we had a problem on our hands.

Even as we stepped onto the concrete at the other side of the road, three hideously disfigured forms appeared.

I didn't want to split the team, but someone had to check through the door and ensure it was safe, while others needed to focus on the looming threat.

"Dove, you get the door. Check carefully, then protect the flank. Jack and I will cover this. Veronica, you stay with them. If anything happens to us, Julia will tell you what to do."

"No," J muttered. "If we split the team—"

"No time." I dropped to my knee, shouldering my rifle and sighting the first dog. "Left."

Jack grunted, likely mirroring my action. "Right."

We fired, the boom resounding up the alley created by the two buildings. Dimly, I noted the sound of the door opening as the first two dogs dropped. Now the growl was joined by the moans. Zombies, and by the sounds of it a large pack.

I rose and stepped back, sighting again, and squeezed the trigger. The third dog had been bounding toward me, but I caught it in the chest, enough to slow it down.

"Come on!" Veronica screamed, and we dashed into the building, then turned back to fasten the door.

I took a second, sucking in a deep breath and feeling the prickle of sweat pooling at the back of my shirt, things I hadn't allowed myself to feel before now. I looked at the door and grimaced. It was wooden and heavy, but if they were motivated... I swallowed heavily. It wouldn't hold for long. What could we do? Even as I glanced around, I spied an old, concrete planter. The greenery had long since died, but it would be heavy. Hopefully, it would do the job.

"Help me." Jack and I dashed over and dragged the wood structure against the door then hurried after the group.

Julia hobbled, leaning heavily on Dave and Allan. "We need to get secured quickly." In her voice I heard resignation. "I'm holding you up."

I knew exactly what she was alluding to and refused to allow that thought to take root. "No way. We're all in this together."

"Leroy—"

"Damien. My name is Damien. Now let's get to the garage. The door is metal and has a lock on the right side. Once there, we can relax and consider what to do next."

I thrust my rifle at Jack and scooped the slight woman up in my arms and strode forward, avoiding the searching, questioning gazes. There'd be time for answers later.

Julia

It felt like I was a liability, hanging onto Leroy. *Damien.* He was strong and made me feel important when I was at my weakest.

Right now, I wasn't much use to anyone. I'd had to make decisions in the past, ones that didn't just impact life but were all about death. I'd been ready to make the sacrifice, yet he'd overruled me. In the stupidest of ways, it showed he valued me.

We weren't out of the woods. There could be zombies even in this building, yet here I was, in his arms.

"I can handle your rifle if you insist on carrying me." God knew, uselessness wasn't an experience I enjoyed.

"It'll be fine." The vibration of his gruff voice took me by surprise.

"I could walk you know." I was too close, it felt too darn intimate.

"No. This way we can move quickly."

Of course Leroy was right; we were moving at a fair pace down the long hallway.

The rest of the team had already gone ahead and were waiting at the door when the crash sounded. "Shit!" Now he bolted, jolting me, and pain shot through my entire leg as I bobbed up and down.

I reached to my back; the holster at the small of my back chafed, but I was thankful I'd kept the small pistol close by. I'd come across it on my first mission, in a house that had been evacuated, among other useful items. My fingers gripped the wood handle tight. "What are you—"

"Just keep running. I'll keep them busy."

With the juggling movements, it was hard to aim, but I squeezed off a shot, and the lead zombie in the pack giving chase went down. I'd hit its leg, and others behind tumbled over it.

Our team was screaming at us to move faster. I heard Leroy panting from exertion as I hit another zombie, but they were closer this time, almost near enough for me to smell them. They swarmed around the fallen, heading in our direction, and the stench of rotting flesh and the heart- pounding dread that iced me over were debilitating.

Hands tugged and pulled at us, the team drawing us to safety before the zombies could lay even a finger on us. The metal door clanged shut as the zombies loomed too close.

"That was too close," panted Leroy, and I had to agree.

He lowered me to the ground, and I lay there, eyes fixed on the concrete ceiling, my chest heaving. Someone shoved a cup of water into my hands, and I took it, drinking deeply as the throb of my leg once more captured my attention.

Dove crouched down beside me. "Shimmy out of the pants so I can get a better look."

Leroy

Too damned close! I'd almost bought it out there with the woman in my arms. The one I didn't want to feel anything for but did. Now Dove was hunkered down beside her, her long pants shucked, and all that covered her modesty was a pair of pink panties.

I tore my eyes away, hoping to clear the cloud that settled in my mind. The motley assortment gathered beyond the sleeping area we'd roughly erected earlier with blankets strung across.

Night was drawing in. The worst time to be out as zombies naturally became active, hunting for survivors.

I rounded up Allan. "Have you seen any other survivors around?"

The shake of his head was slow, and I wondered what he wasn't telling us.

"What can you tell us then?"

He hunkered down, chewing slowly on the jerky he'd been offered. "We're the only country affected. New Zealand had a couple of early cases, but they were neutralized before the virus could spread. All other developing countries washed their hands, because the situation was too grave for them to take a chance. There have even been a couple of cases at sea, so no boats will dock here. We're on our own until we get on top of the virus."

"Holy fuck!"

Everyone stared at Allan, and I wondered how much truth there was in what he said, and yet... "How do you know this?"

"I had people who knew people in Parliament House. Some intercepted information, and others were in senior positions until the pre-virus purge."

The purge was where a number of high-ranking ministers and their teams had been replaced in the weeks leading up to the virus taking hold of the population. It had been huge news—blasted out over the internet, television, and radios that ministers were sacked and replaced with others without any reason. Joining the dots was easy now in hindsight. Agriculture, Science Research and Development, and even Health portfolios had seen a massive upheaval, and now we knew why.

"So, these people who took on the roles? They were tied to the prime minister—"

Allan shook his head. "The prime minister didn't know. Those who replaced the heads were of the other persuasion."

"Then—"

"The prime minister was overthrown once they were sequestered in a remote location. That's all I know on that front. What I do know is they'd been covertly testing vaccines on service personnel with limited success. The virus release was a major cock-up as it wasn't ready for release because the vaccines weren't working properly, but they needed to speed up the timeframe. They released virus to the public, and there were catastrophic results. There is also talk that there is more than one Patient Zero."

Allan's telling shrug chilled my guts.

The sound of hobbling caught my attention, and J, together with Dove, joined us around the circle. "What have you learned?"

She lowered herself down slowly, grimacing all the way, in the center of the group, and Jack passed her a plate of food. Dove accepted another. One was thrust into my hands, but I stared at it. "Allan was saying the PM didn't know, and someone in power replaced all the high- level pollies who were purged. They started the virus, and the situation got out of hand real quick. The worst is there's not just one place where the virus originated."

J grunted and scooped up some re-heated stew. "Doesn't surprise me really. But if that's the case, why didn't you say something, Allan?"

I could feel the tension running between them but waited to hear his answer.

"I worked for the government, Julia. I was bound by the Official Secrets Act until the dissolution of the government. Then I promised the camp commanders I'd keep it quiet until we found whatever research was left."

Abby and Helen, J's sister and mother, joined the group. They slid down to the cold concrete, sitting beside the small fire, and J's face lit up like a Christmas tree. "It feels like a dream to see you both alive. I thought... When I couldn't find you..."

Tears dribbled down her cheeks, and she slid her plate to the floor, wiping them away with her hand. Inside my chest there was a lump that settled heavily. I didn't doubt others were feeling the effects of this miracle reunion too.

"We can talk later, Julia. Once we're safe. Allan says there's a camp only a few days away, and we need to head there."

I swiveled toward the man. "We were told to return."

"And you will. But first we need to get Abby and Helen to a secure location, and I want to offload these serums. The camp is on the outskirts of town, about two days on foot. They've built a farm in an old school, and there's proper housing. A doctor too."

I glanced at J to see the flattening of her lips. "We have a mission to complete—"

"And I'm over-ruling you, Julia. Check in with your commander and he'll tell you I can do that."

"Bastard." She rose and retreated with a fast hobble. I couldn't help but watch her leave and wonder if this tension was a precursor of the next few days.

Chapter 4

Julia

THE NEXT COUPLE of days were among the hardest I'd experienced since the outbreak of the virus.

Abby and Mum were alive. I'd lost then regained my entire family. I couldn't really call Allan family though, more like an intruder who Mum acted like a new bride around. She fawned like she'd done straight after their wedding. *Hell, I had too.* In my defense, I'd only been ten when they married soon after Dad died. I'd been pleased she'd found love again after nursing Dad who passed from the big C.

Now I questioned Allan's motives and actions. Abby was over the moon, but she was only thirteen, and her Dad and Mum were in the same place, both alive and neither zombified. In these days, that was no mean feat. Actually, it took on the status of a miracle, and for some reason everyone—except me and Leroy—accepted this at face value.

Stuck on the back of the dray, I swayed, watched for zombies, and my brain moved through the confusing mass of emotions I rarely allowed myself to consider.

Then there was Leroy. Damien Leroy, it turned out.

He'd saved me, even when I'd been prepared to give it all up to save the others. One hell of a sharpshooter and a leader. I'd seen that in the way he stepped up after I'd been injured.

We crept along the road, the clop of the horses' hooves echoing, with Dove at the reins. Everyone except me walked, and I felt down-right foolish.

"How much further?" Abby whined, and I smiled. I'd take that whine any day of the week over her death.

I glanced over my shoulder and saw the large fencing, glinting in the distance as it surrounded a clutch of houses. "Not far now, Abs."

"My feet hurt," she said, and I sighed.

"Hey, Dove, can we carry Abby for the rest of the way?"

He nodded after taking a moment to think, stopped the dray, and my little sister climbed up beside me.

"Sit next to Dove, Abs. Just in case we need to engage zombies. I need to be able to see a full three-sixty."

Abs nodded, but before she climbed along the length of the dray she bent down with a deep frown. "You've changed, Julia."

That hurt. I'd changed because I had to. Sure, she had too, but there was still a level of innocence, and I wondered how she'd managed to foster that in these dangerous times. Instead of dwelling, I shifted my rifle and glanced out. Something moved behind us. I squinted and swore, scooped up the binoculars and peered. "Fuck! Incoming. Let's move it up, people."

We'd had a pretty quiet ride since leaving the heart of Canberra, but with people here now, zombies naturally gravitated near the living.

The team snapped into formation, those unarmed or incapable of fighting—including my mother—in the center, the armed on the perimeter.

We weren't that far away from the settlement, and yet safety never seemed further away. The pack on our tail was growing and moving quickly.

"Mum, get on the dray." I reached out and pulled her up, Leroy hoisting her. "Get up near Abs." I rose now, shifted around, and braced myself against one of the metal feed drums. "Move faster," I yelled and aimed with the rifle.

Dove gee'd the horses, and the movement of the platform made sighting pretty close to impossible. The team was moving at a trot now, Jack moving backward while Van hurried the scientists along. Thankfully, during our break in Canberra he'd gotten himself back under control, but I was aware he'd need help before ever being included in a patrol again.

We drew level with the fencing as voices started calling to us. "Up here," they yelled, and our team sped up, running now for the gate which opened halfway.

Just when I was sure we'd all make it a scream captured my attention, and I watched as Jack dropped, a zombie clutching him. The movements slowed to a frame-by-frame speed, and I watched the bite. The spurt of blood.

"No!" I aimed and fired. The zombie spun and fell to the ground. "Jack!"

Even as I attempted to jump from the dray Leroy was there, pushing me back. "It's too late. You know that."

"But he's one of my team!" I strained against him, my heartbeat a frenetic pound.

"It's too late, J. He'll turn. One. Hundred. Percent. You know that."

I did, and it rent me apart, pain ricocheting through my chest. Hot tears scoured my cheeks. "Jack!"

I heard his screams now. Panicked. Desperate. The sound of a man aware of his fate. We'd dealt with enough to know exactly what came next. After all, we'd seen it time and again, every one of us. Either they tore him apart or he became a zombie. The zombies descended on him, and I turned away. I had to accept defeat and the loss of one of my team. A man who left a family behind. One I'd have to notify personally. I swallowed hard as the bitter taste of sickness filled my mouth.

"I'll deal with it."

I knew what that meant, and I stuffed my fingers in my ears, horrified. The sound, the loud and echoing boom, told me everything I needed to know, and I dropped to the wooden base, sobbing.

We were ushered through the gate and shuffled into the back area. Dove quietly set about the task of unharnessing the horses and releasing them from the cage while Abby and my mother hovered with Van and the two scientists. Allan demanded to talk to the leader in charge, and Leroy watched me in silence as I climbed off the dray.

I looked into Leroy's eyes and saw the compassion there. "I can't... I have to tell his family. What the hell do I tell them?"

"You tell them what you've told me. He was a good man. One who gave everything to protect his family. You tell them he was brave."

Leroy

J was a mess. Not that it was unexpected. Every leader took the loss of those under their command as an assault on themselves. She'd found a quiet spot and cried—ugly, ripping sounds—while I stood guard, allowing her some dignity as she mourned. I waited patiently until the storm passed. The sounds of her clearing her face, wiping away the tears, and rebalancing herself.

When she emerged, she looked tired but composed, only the red of her nose and eyes betraying the devastation she now hid. "Thanks, Leroy."

"You're welcome."

She turned around. "Don't say anything about that, okay? I mean, I need to be in control around everyone else. They rely on me."

I wondered if she realized no one would think less of her if they'd known she'd fallen apart, but I kept my thoughts to myself. After all, I was only here for a short time. I had no intention of hanging around.

"Well, we should go find some food," I said. "Liam said to meet in the back courtyard."

Julia sniffled and sighed. "Yes. Let's go eat."

She strode ahead of me, shoulders firm and spine ramrod straight, and even though she still hobbled, there was a dignity about her. From the rear you'd believe her wholly unconcerned with the loss of a team member. She was a true enigma to my mind, and I wondered how much more she'd rise through the camp ranks.

We entered what had once been a series of backyards, sheds dotted here and there, along with some posts which had been part of the previous fencing. Liam—the head of the compound—and his wife, Elaine, smiled in welcome. J took Elaine's hand and murmured something. I trailed the trio to what appeared to be the leaders' table and scanned the crowd, noting the rest of our party dotted throughout the throng.

Liam cleared his throat, and the collective group quieted, taking their seats as did we. "Our men have attended to your man, Jack. He'll be cremated in the morning and his ashes scattered in the garden with the rest of our losses. His sacrifice will never be in vain." Liam spoke loudly, ensuring everyone heard, and I watched the way J's knuckles turned white, though her countenance didn't betray her emotions.

When Liam sat, she rose. "Thank you for your kind words, Liam. We appreciate your hospitality, the opportunity to rest, and above all, that your people were prepared to take the risk to retrieve Jack's body. He was a good man. A father and husband who only ever wanted to protect those he loved. A great friend, warrior, and team member. He will be missed by all whom he met."

The crowd was silent for a moment, their heads bowed in memory of those we'd lost. One by one, as the moment of solemnity passed, the crowd turned to their small groups, and the chatter rose.

"You're welcome to stay here as long as you wish," Liam said, and J turned to him, her face pale but composed.

"Thanks, but I need to get Allan back to base."

The conversation ended as vegetables were passed around, with succulent pork. *It's been far too long since I've eaten like this*, I thought, helping myself to a portion.

At the end of the meal, J headed to the sleeping area we'd been allocated as a team. Not for the first time, I wondered what motivated her, except for the loss of her family and her loyalty to her friends. If we'd met earlier... I snatched that thought back, memories of the ring in my pocket scorching my heart and brain.

If only... Two words I refused to utter.

Julia

I woke early. The sound of birdsong driving me back to the old life I'd enjoyed. The one pre-zombies. The team continued to sleep as I picked my way through the camp we'd set up in the living room.

It was only when I opened the door that reality hit. This idyll offered us a home.

"I wish," I muttered. It would be perfect. Quiet and welcoming. No pressure or daily incursions from zombies. Liam had told us they rarely saw them now.

I sat down on the steps, looked out across what had been the asphalt roadway and across to the now dilapidated buildings. The door opened, and I turned, made to rise, but it was Leroy, with two steaming cups in hand.

"I saw you come out here. Thought you could do with some coffee."

I watched, my brain reminding me that he was young, athletic, and *sexy*. I tried really hard to curb the last thought, but as always it zinged into my mind.

"Mind if I join you?"

At my nod, he joined me on the step, passing the steaming cup to me, and I felt the frisson of connection as our hands glanced against each other.

"It's going to be a lovely day." He spoke quietly.

My smile bloomed. "Yeah. Perfect for traveling in a dray."

He laughed, and the sound ricocheted through me. "You've got this dry sense of humor, you know?"

That killed my mirth. "Perhaps, but we've got to get Allan back to the base. Whatever he has on those computers and papers, they're needed urgently."

"And the serums?"

"I think Ramon, Liam's brother, co-opted them. He's an epidemiologist, so this kind of stuff is what he was trained to deal with."

"Huh. But you're worried."

I nodded. "We didn't see a lot of movement until we got here. The zombies are congregating in certain areas, just like we've done. It's like they—as much as us—need each other. It feels... I dunno, odd? Did you notice the way the dogs and the zombies were together? Not attacking or..."

Until now, I hadn't been able to quantify why this felt odd. What appeared off and disquieting. But suddenly it made sense that they were forming enclaves. Those of mindless, flesh-eating individuals. I shuddered.

"You've considered what you just said?" The worry was clear in his tone.

"Yeah. It frightens the life out of me. I mean, why? What possible aim could there be for them to congregate?"

I couldn't help but notice the way Leroy's eyebrows drew together above the bridge of his nose or how the wrinkles at the corners of his eyes deepened.

"Strength in numbers? They're learning to attack en masse?"

Nausea rose at his words. "Surely not?"

"They don't attack a heavily armed outpost. In fact, there were only a few uncoordinated attacks until we reached here, then there was a nest. They didn't attempt to hit on the fence, simply went for the travelers. What does that say?"

A greasy knot formed in my belly. "We need to round up the team and get out of here." I rose, but Leroy reached out and grabbed my hand.

"Liam offered us alternative transport. They have an old,

shielded bus, a fortified horse float, and truck. They'll take us back later today. It's all arranged."

For a moment a shaft of anger blazed. I nearly demanded that he stop arranging everything, because I was the leader, but the words died before reaching my mouth. He was right. We'd be there in a matter of hours instead of days. We'd all arrive safely.

"Are we all..." I couldn't finish, because I'd caught sight of Abby and my mother settling in last night. Talking dresses and hair. I wondered when was the last time they'd had that kind of companionship. Or conversation.

"Allan's returning here after he's completed his mission, whatever that is. Your mother and Abby have already elected to remain here."

"Oh." There didn't seem much else to say. "Well, we should get the team up. Tell them what's happening." And I needed to say goodbye. Properly this time, in case it was also the last one.

Chapter 5

Leroy

I WATCHED as J spoke with the team. When she'd briefed them prior to the mission, I hadn't felt any real connection with any of them. This time, she was just as brief, but I could read the nuances of her. The way she looked at each member of her team, as if committing their faces to memory. She didn't mention her mother or sister, but Allan was spoken of with a brief hesitation, and her hands balled, white-knuckled.

"Liam and Elaine have made available the services of a bus and a truck, plus a reinforced horse float. We'll be home in hours instead of the three days we'd originally plotted."

Most of the team signaled relief, with smiles and nods. Only Dove didn't. Instead, there was an odd hesitation in his manner. *I'll investigate that later*, I thought.

"We leave in a couple of hours, but until then, I have a list of some tasks you could complete for the camp. They're not going to take a long time, so once completed we'll meet back here."

She sent them off to join with members of the camp who'd take them about assigned duties until only J, Dove, and myself remained.

"Dove, there's been a request for a couple of marriages and some baptisms. The members are looking only for private affairs, which is why they didn't request it last night."

He frowned. "I don't have robes or..."

J smiled. "Liam and Elaine were on top of that. They found a church nearby and searched—is it called the vestry? They found robes and books they thought you'd appreciate. Plus, a registry book if that helps."

Dove blinked once, twice. "It's called the sacristy. And yes, I'll perform the ceremonies, but I haven't celebrated either in a long time. Not since..."

J reached out a hand, and for the first time a dark emotion slid through me. *Jealousy.* Why didn't make any sense, just that it was there. "It's okay. But these people are believers, and they need you now. They need the faith that's part of you."

Liam entered the room, a box in his arms. "I hope this is everything you need. We got a chalice and some wine. There wasn't much left, and the church was a mess. Someone had ransacked it, but these were in a cupboard and obviously not high on anyone's list of necessary items."

Dove accepted the box, treating it like the most valuable gift. "Thank you," he said tremulously.

Once they'd left the room, I sidled up to J. "What's Dove's story? I get he was a priest but..."

"He was in the hospital giving last rites when the lockdown occurred. He taught in the private school nearby but took his turn on a roster. A week or so later, he was pressed into assisting with one of the early hunts for goods and uninfected. He came across a bunch of the girls from his school, but they'd become zombies. The others in the team had to pull him away as he tried to give them last rites. After that, we realized that while he had many skills, he couldn't, under normal circumstances, be called upon for anything that requires him to fight. We include him in the teams because he's a reasonable medic, good with animals, and for the emotional support he can offer."

Listening to her expounding the man's positive traits, the green emotion bit a little more sharply.

"He likes you." The words just kind of slid out.

J sighed. "I know. Before you ask, he also knows I know. We discussed it a couple of months ago, but I'm not..." She bit her lip. "I'm not sure what I want other than for the world to return to normal. Or at least our country, which it seems is the only one with a rampant infection."

Her words tweaked the questioning section of my mind. Australia had been a mostly stable and calm country, so why would they release this virus here and not everywhere else? And why... I cut that thought off before it could form.

"Why only Australia though? I mean, if it's a plot with terroristic leanings, you would expect this would be released worldwide." That idea burned me deep inside.

"I don't know, but I rather think Allan might. But for now, let's just get through the next few hours." She stalked off at with a loose hobble, and I let her go, with no task or the future of one for the first time in a while.

Eventually Dove returned, in his gown and stole, and the families and couples filed in. The service took place while Liam and Elaine used a camera to take photos. Then, with the deed done, the families trotted back out.

Liam caught my eye and beckoned me over. "J said you were an itinerant. I was wondering where you were heading next."

I shrugged. "I hadn't really planned anything yet. Why?"

He offered me a seat, and I settled in. "I have a number of younger members who need to be taught the basics of combat. We have some older members, mainly ex-soldiers and the odd police officer." He shrugged. "But I need a trainer for the younger generation. If this is going to be our new existence, I want the people here to be safe into the future. To be able to man the gates and watch towers and keep us safe from the zombie waves. To protect what we've built. If you're looking for somewhere to stay for a while, or even put down roots, we'd love for you to join us."

That had my throat tightening. I hadn't considered permanency in so long. Not since— I took a moment to suck in a steadying breath. "I'll certainly consider it."

Julia

Leroy settled himself in beside me, and I was uncomfortably aware of him. His scent and his overall presence. It wasn't as though I hadn't sat next to a man since the invasion, or for that matter had a lover. I'd had a couple of brief encounters that hadn't really overwhelmed me, but something about Damien Leroy grabbed my attention like a dog with a bone. Just being next to him set off some kind of internal alarm system in my body, and it was difficult to ignore the instinctive reaction.

Instead, I settled on looking out through the window, hoping to calm the sudden giddiness and erratic heartbeat. Not to mention the damned heating of parts of my body! Once we were loaded up and the truck pulled out with our horses, we would follow the other vehicle. Liam had included a crack team of seven to keep both vehicles secure from any ambush.

The engine revved and excitement grew. I didn't look back. Mum and Abby were already over at the old school section of the encampment, setting up their home in one of the hastily erected shed houses that had sprung up in certain locations around their camp. Elaine had explained they'd come across kits in a warehouse and had appropriated them for family habitation and erected as many as they could so when newcomers or new families needed them, they were ready.

I'd said goodbye to my sister, who still appeared untouched by the reality of the zombie invasion, and my mother, who assured me Allan would return to her soon. She hadn't made any requests of me and I felt at arm's length. All in all, it was a strange and unsatisfactory situation, but I had a role to fulfill. A team to lead and a commitment to keep.

My reverie was smashed as the gears of the bus ground and we lurched forward. I reached out and grabbed the bar in front of me.

"These old clunkers never rode well," muttered Leroy, and I couldn't stop myself from glancing at him.

"You know about them?"

"I drove them for a while before I joined the army in Townsville. The gears are shit."

I blinked. He'd just shared far more than he'd ever done before with me, and I felt a kind of connection. "Were you in Townsville when this..."

It was always hard to say 'the virus breakout', so I usually avoided it. But he appeared to understand, and he shook his head.

"No. I was in Brisbane at the time they made all the announcements, and my... The news came through and I tried to get home. I made it eventually. Between the state of the roads and trying to get hold of resources, it took three weeks to get there. By the time I arrived, everyone— " He cleared his throat, and I waited, unwilling to break the spell. "Everyone was gone or dead. There didn't seem much to stay for, and I heard things were worse the further south you went. Especially once you got past Brisbane. So, a group of us who were left, headed out, planning to help clear up the mess." Leroy shrugged, and I decided it was best to leave it alone for now, but I wondered what happened to the rest of the crew he'd set off with.

Silence descended on us, and for the first time, as we trundled down the road and as I gazed over the landscape, the reality of the losses hit home. "I didn't realize..."

Leroy grunted. "We came to Canberra through as much of the unpopulated areas as we could, but the bus and truck travel better on the roads. We'll get a better idea of the devastation this way."

Cars and trucks filled the roads. Remains—little more than bones—littered them too. Every mile unwrapped more death and carnage. While I'd known our area was certainly a hot zone, this amplified that knowledge. I realized quickly enough we weren't taking any of the main roads and asked the driver why.

"We've gotten reports that the zombies have taken over sections, waiting in overturned vehicles and making it impossible to get through. This way, since we're traveling with the horse and truck and moving slow, it's better and safer. Not so many roadblocks, and it keeps us away from the worst of the hot spots. It's slower, but even with all the reinforcing, by going the other way we can't be sure we'd reach our destination intact."

Most of my missions had taken place in the Queanbeyan section by choice, and I hadn't heard this sort of intel previously. It was sobering. I glanced back out the window.

I don't know exactly what I expected as we entered the beginning final stretch some two hours after leaving the camp in Chisholm. The overpass wasn't a section I'd traversed in months. We'd usually moved into the more residential zones, looking for equipment, food supplies, and anything that would ensure the comfort of our residents.

The driver pulled the bus to a stop about half a kilometer away, with the truck driver doing the same. The two drivers hopped out, conferred, then returned to their vehicles. Once our driver was back in his seat, he turned toward us, and my guts tightened at the look on his face.

"All right, boys and girls. This is the hairy part. Underpasses are notorious hang-outs for the reanimated zombies, and they like to drop down and take passengers by surprise, so look alive. We're going to gun the vehicles and move as fast as we can, but chances are good we'll come under a sustained attack. Do not open any windows, and close any you have open now. I have retrofitted a mirror to the roof, through a plexiglass casing. I'll get an accurate look at any combatants on the roof, so wait for my heads-up before attempting to fire on any zombies or noises."

I picked up my rifle and checked it. "Clear." The echo through the cabin reminded me once again that we were in the middle of a war zone.

He grunted, restarted the engine, and flashed the vehicle ahead. Now they rumbled forward, increasing their speed, and the bus rattled and shook.

I got my first look at the overpass and almost swallowed my tongue at seeing the heads pop up.

Dove, in the seat opposite Leroy and myself, pulled on his scarf and began to pray, murmuring and making symbols in the air. I knew under normal circumstances he'd be shaking his dipper with holy water or oil, but since we were inside the bus with the windows closed, he merely pointed.

Rolling under the bridge, I heard the first thud, the scratch of nails grappling onto the metal of the roof, and the sounds of scurrying above us. Unnerved, I swallowed, the gulp audible, and my gaze collided with Leroy's.

"We're safe," he assured me, but I wasn't so sure.

After long seconds that stretched interminably, we drove back out into bright sunshine, and the driver called out, "Two, middle of the vehicle."

One of the guards at the back opened a reinforced sunroof, and he and another shooter filled the hole. Two loud bangs echoed, thuds sounded, and they dropped down, closing the roof swiftly. "Got them!" one called.

In the large side mirror, I caught sight of two bodies dropping to the ground. Just as I started to breathe easy, a hand squirreled up my window. Long, black nails attached to a scabby, gray arm. "Holy shit! One here," I yelled.

Someone else called out a similar statement, and I stood up as the creature on my side crawled up the side of the bus until it clung before me, nails sliding down between the rim and window.

I heard windows slide open, heard twin booms, and watched as black-red blood sprayed. The creature fell away but not before I'd seen the eyes, yellow-red orbs that sent frigid shocks through my system.

We trundled on, but the horror of that view stuck with me, and even as we rolled into the grounds of the hospital I wondered, for the first time, if I was done as a warrior.

Leroy

I'd seen J's reaction to the zombie in the window. She'd paled, her eyes unfocused, and when she slumped back to the seat, as much as I wanted to comfort her, I knew it would be hypocritical. After all, I had been part of the system that allowed this to take place.

When the bus stopped, I kept silent, moved away and into the building until Allan got off. I indicated I needed a word, and he stared at me. "What?"

There was no time left for hesitation, so I inhaled. "You need intel, and I have some."

"What?" His gaze roamed my face, as if checking to see if I was serious.

"Inside." I gestured with my thumb, then headed directly for the cafeteria, not that I'd tell him there, but I needed coffee before I spilled the beans.

"What do you know?" he asked.

"Coffee first, then I think the commandant's office would be the best place for this discussion."

"Now," he demanded, but I shook it off. What I had to say wasn't going to be easy or pretty. So I hurried off, grabbed a mug, then determinedly made my way to the office.

J was sitting outside, likely waiting to make her report, and for the first time, my decision to tell all wavered. I had nothing to personally gain, yet explaining why and how became vitally important if I had any hopes of coming to terms with my part in the mess, so I settled in beside her.

"What are you doing here?" she asked.

"Well, I have to confess, I know more about the outbreak than most would guess."

Her eyes widened. "What do you know?"

Allan rounded the corner, the commandant at his side. "Leroy?"

"Sir, in your office would be best." I stood up and strode into the small room. Better to be on the offensive, because I sure as hell didn't know how they'd treat me when this was done if I didn't bull my way in.

J followed, and I wondered how she'd react, then sighed. It was too late for regrets. Once the door closed, they all turned and looked at me.

"The virus was planted through certain applications to the water system. A group of about fifty of us were recruited for a special mission by an ASIO operative through standard military procedures. At the time we didn't know it was a virus. We were informed it was a top- level security vaccine that needed covert deployment. Those of us chosen to spread it were injected with a different strain, they said 'just in case of mutation', but their testing proved it would be an unlikely outcome. We were kept in isolation for three weeks then each sent to a variety of locations. I was sent to Brisbane. Every state except Tasmania was treated, because they said the flow through from traffic across Bass Strait would make it unnecessary. I have the documentation they gave us."

I reached into my backpack, removed the small, brown envelope I'd carried since the beginning, and handed it to Allan.

"It's not a lot, but there's a list of contacts and the process for spreading the inoculation into the water source there. Plus, another contact for after the fact. Once I realized what was happening, I ran. I saw the media reports where they stated someone escaped and was Patient Zero, but I knew that wasn't right. I ran as fast as I could, hoping to halt its spread and seek the assistance of the head of the project, but he was dead. They told me in Townsville that he had committed suicide. I also had private reasons for returning, but it was too late." Memories of Katrina, the zombie woman I'd been engaged to, circled through my mind. The thud of the bullet hitting her skull was a sound I revisited in my dreams nightly.

J made a noise, somewhere between a hiccup and a soggy snuffle, and I closed my eyes. I knew the revulsion she was likely feeling. I'd seen it in my own eyes for the first couple of months after the virus outbreak. I knew I'd been used, and that scalded me. "Allan secured information about—"

"You knew about this? Even when you came here?" The commandant halted my words, fury infusing every sound.

"I did. Once I grasped what the mission was about, I was thankful." I now stood rigidly to attention. They'd probably shoot me, or out me, and I deserved nothing less.

"Kevin, he's giving us everything he knows, and that might be helpful to the cause. We use his contacts and knowledge along with what I've retrieved. What else can you tell us, Leroy?"

"The plan was political. Came out of one of the departments, which you already know. He worked with the ASIO operative and chose us. Made the arrangements through our CO for the secondment."

"Allan?"

"We knew a lot about that, but hadn't managed to find any surviving operatives thus far." Allan circled the desk and sat down, the chair squeaking beneath him as he sighed. "The information I brought has the DNA sequencing of the virus, and the strains these boys were inoculated with. Just not the names of those involved."

The commandant shook his head. "We can't share this, otherwise Leroy—"

"They'd kill him," J piped up. "We need to keep him out in the field until we can undertake damage mitigation." I stared at her, and she shrugged. "Middle-management training comes in handy these days."

"We should go through our findings then strategize," intoned the commandant, and J nodded.

Foolish though it was, a wave of relief washed over me. They weren't going to shoot me or cast me out. For now, that was enough. It just remained to be seen what would happen next.

Chapter 6

Julia

I LAY ON MY BED, listening to Leroy's breathing. He'd dropped to sleep pretty quickly after we'd settled into the small room that was mine. At least I think he had. Allan, the commandant, and I, reluctantly agreed that he needed to be supervised. For his safety, in case the truth got out. Until we could relocate to a safe location.

Actually, I was thankful he was sleeping, because the conflicting emotions inside me were too damn confusing for me to deal with the added stress of him personally! First, I had to come to terms with the fact that he'd been involved in the whole zombie apocalypse thing. Then came my attraction—because that's exactly what this was—complete with wanting to jump on him at any given time. Then came him. His proximity to me, the scent and size. That he made me feel safe.

"I'm not a retiring wallflower," I muttered then stilled, shocked as he turned and opened his eyes.

"No, you're not, J."

Oh God! My body began that warming, firming, hungry thing, and I wanted to melt into a pile of goo in front of him. *Nuh-uh!*

"I wasn't talking to you," I said.

He smiled, and a dimple made an appearance in one cheek. *Fuck! I am totally screwed!* I wanted those lips on mine, and even more, I wanted that body—that body, naked—in this bed and twined around me. Holding me. Loving me.

"You're no flower that wilts, but you are a woman. A beautiful and strong warrior. A leader. And I want you, Julia."

It was the first time he'd said my name, and he made it a caress. My gaze roamed over him, from the tight-fitting shirt that clung to his muscular chest to the bulge in his pants.

The gulp I swallowed gave away the emotions roiling inside me, because I saw the way his gaze moved to my throat, then his smile broadened.

"I could come over there." His breathy words stole my senses, and I watched him slide off his bed and advanced toward me on mine.

All I could do was wait as the tiger prowled toward me, my mouth dry and my body burning with sexual hunger.

"I...I want you, Leroy. But I'm not sure I trust you."

That stopped him in his tracks. He flinched, and I felt bad, but I had to be honest. Nothing else was acceptable to me.

"Why?"

I must have looked like a gaping fish, mouth open. "I... Uh...."

"The virus." He threw the words at me, like hurled abuse. "I get it. But I won't apologize, J. I was doing my job." Now he spoke stiffly, as if each word was a cinder block in his mouth. Sitting up, I turned and let my feet dangle over the side of the bed, needing to feel equal.

A silly thing of course, as I was his team leader, but still. "Look, we all lost a lot of people in this, and passions and emotions are difficult to set aside. Maybe it doesn't feel like it should matter or whatever, but if and when we make love, I want to know it's with a man I respect."

God! Talk about taking a foot out of your mouth and replacing it with another!

"Fine." He stomped back to his bed. "You're sure you can

manage sharing a room with me then?" He sounded peevish, and I guess I couldn't blame him, but still his words shredded my emotions.

He lay down and turned his back to me.

Fuck. Fuck. Fuckety fuck!

"Don't be like that," I cajoled, but he didn't turn around.

It was ages before I lay down again and allowed myself to fall into a fitful sleep.

Leroy

Waking in the morning, it was with the knowledge that I was a pariah. I mean, I'd known from the beginning that when I shared what I knew, I'd be unwelcome, but that J didn't trust me, speared me. Scoured my insides so they ached and bled continuously. I'd never experienced that before.

All of which was inexplicable. After all, I'd known this woman less than a week, and somehow, she'd become more important than Katrina? "No way." I'd just make myself stop caring and wondering. That would solve the issue, and I'd move on as soon as possible. In fact...

The thought bloomed, and I rose, pleased J was still asleep. I hastily tossed my few possessions into my backpack, keeping my actions as quiet as possible. My hand was on the door when she spoke. "Where are you going?"

The sound of her voice, sleep-roughened, had me turning in surprise. I should have known better, because she was heavy-lidded and her hair was mussy. *Enticing.*

"Leaving. I don't belong here."

J rubbed at her eyes. "None of us do, but we need you, Leroy."

Her words stilled me in my tracks. For all of a second the warmth that had dissipated during the night returned. Then the reality of her words intruded. *Not because they need me so much as what I know.*

"I have to leave."

"Maybe, but not until we find some place safe to stash you. I mean, there's too much ill feeling here."

"I planned on joining Liam and Elaine."

J squinted. "What?"

"They offered me a place. A role helping teach their younger members self-defense and so on."

The silence had me wondering what was going on in J's mind. "I see. You were just going to leave. Not tell anyone, including me." Hurt echoed in her words, and I nearly laughed out loud at my stupidity in thinking she'd care.

"Come on, J. You said it yourself last night, you don't trust me."

She screwed up her face, a delightful move, but it pierced me, and I had to remind myself 'do not care or react'. That, it appeared, was easier said than done.

"J and Leroy to the commandant's office. J and Leroy." The echo of the intercom broke the fraught moment, and I was thankful for that.

I grasped my backpack and swung it over my shoulder. J jumped out of the bed, scraped back her masses of hair, and tamed it with an elastic band.

"We'll discuss this later," she warned. I shrugged. I didn't plan on staying.

Julia

The commandant paced as I outlined the problem. "He's got no intention of staying, and I think...actually, I'm fairly sure that any attempts on our part to find another safe house will result in him disappearing. The best chance we have of keeping track is to release him to Liam and Elaine's camp."

"But we need information that only he has, J. Is there some way you can convince him?"

I saw that look in his eye, speculation followed by calculation. I wanted to smack the man but simply balled my fists, stood my ground, and answered with a firm, "No! No, I think sending him there means we can keep track, and that's the best option open to us currently."

The commandant sighed and turned. I knew he was planning and plotting. I just wondered what else he had in mind, given the way his thinking had just turned.

When he turned back his face was pained. "All right then, but you go with him. I need someone I can trust there. Besides which, there aren't any members of our coalition on-site. You could liaise with Liam and Elaine, bring them into the fold."

Now, I'm no one's fool, least of all the commandant's. "Sir, I'm not sure they're interested in joining sides—"

"But I didn't ask what you thought. I need you there to sell the coalition to them. Do it, J, or I'm not sure there'll be a place here for you."

Poleaxed didn't even begin to describe my emotions. "Sir?"

"Dismissed, J."

I stepped blindly into the corridor, shutting the door behind me, while attempting to make some kind of sense out of what he'd said. *Not sure there'll be a place for you...* I'd given so much to this damned camp. I'd bled and worked and slaved. Fought and *killed*!

In that moment, I understood. I was expendable. It sat poorly, but it also made the decision for me. "I'm going," I murmured, and it was like a great weight lifted off my shoulders.

I turned to find Dove there, frowning. "Where are you going?"

"I'm leaving the camp. Going to Liam and Elaine's, along with Leroy."

He blinked slowly. "Why?"

The laugh I offered was mirthless. "Because I'm expendable, and I want more for myself."

Dove's frown deepened. "Can I come with you?"

The words stopped me in my tracks. "What? Why?"

"Because you're the only one who understood why I don't fight. That even with that, I have skills to offer. They won't let me simply serve God, I have to be *useful* here. On their terms. At Liam and Elaine's, they didn't care about that. They accepted my skills as a medic, but it was my pastoral side I was able to practice. They need me more than I'm required here. Please?"

"I..." At a loss, I didn't know what to say for a moment, then I nodded. "Sure. Why not? We better find Liam's team though and let them know we intend to travel back with them."

Dove shadowed me into the cafeteria where the men were gathering, clearly ready to leave. "Wait!" I called, and the bus driver turned to look at me.

"Hey, we're just about to head out."

"Have you got room for three passengers? We want to come with you." Here and now wasn't the time to explain the whys and wherefores.

The man jittered from leg to leg. "Well, probably, but I need to be gone in the next half hour or so."

I nodded. "Sure. Just let us get organized. Where do you want us to meet you?"

The man scratched his head. "Thirty minutes back here?"

"You got it. Don't go without us."

I knew exactly where Leroy was. I'd told him to stay in the room, and I scurried back there, knowing Dove was also rushing to his small room just down the hall. Bursting through the door, I spied Leroy, book in hand.

"Help me pack. Dove and I are coming with you to Liam and Elaine's. I'll explain on the way."

His face blanked, and he nodded. I remembered he was military, so no doubt used to taking orders without question. I tugged out the small backpack I had on hand. I didn't have much, which was great because there wasn't a lot of space. In minutes we'd stashed everything, and I pulled him through the door.

I didn't look back, because I needed the finality. The closure, I guess. But the sound of our boot-shod feet tromping down the hallway fed the excitement building inside my chest.

This was the right decision. I knew it in my veins.

Leroy

So maybe I was intrigued by J's statement that she was coming with me. Maybe she didn't quite hold what I'd done against me, I considered, as we hurried down the hallway toward the cafeteria. I noted the way the men were watching us as we entered the large room. They didn't rise, and it seemed strange.

"Why aren't they ready to go?"

J turned to me. "Dove is coming with us."

Dove? The priest? "What? *Why?*"

The shake of J's head sent wisps of hair flying, where it had sprung free from her restrained plait. Lust punched me hard, and I swallowed and stepped back.

"What?" J's gaze and the utterance brought me back to reality. *Barely.*

"Uh, Dove? He's coming with us?"

J gave me a look that quieted any further questions. "Because he needs to do something. I'll explain later."

Obviously, there was more to this story than she was able to share right here and now.

But hell, I was used to that, and since I didn't see any real danger from her comments, I shrugged. I would ask again on the bus.

"Your call," I muttered as the man in question joined us, two large rucksacks and a backpack in hand.

"Sorry, had to make sure I had everything," Dove said in a quiet tone.

"Well, since we're all here, let's get moving," the driver said, and we filed behind him toward the door.

Gazes locked on us, and some of the looks sent our way were questioning. When the woman, Casey from catering, came racing down the hall, I smelled a rat. She and Casey were tight, I'd already deduced. If she didn't know, then it was a secret, and those were dangerous.

"J? Where you going? I didn't see a team call-up."

J reached out. "I'm taking a transfer for now, Casey. But I'm

sure we'll meet again." There was genuine sorrow in her voice, and
I noted the strength of the hug she gave, the way the small lines at
the corners of her mouth deepened.

What the hell is going on?

"Be safe, J. That's all I'll ask."

J nodded. "I will." Then J urged us forward into the bright
sunshine and onto the buses. We trundled out, the truck once more
taking up the forward position, and the guards littered between the
two vehicles. At the approach to the overpass, everyone moved into
high alert. But either because it was early in the day, barely nine
AM, or the zombies hadn't regrouped—likely, I'd never know the
answer to that—the number of zombies at that point was minimal,
and none made it onto the bus or truck.

J relaxed after that, and she and Dove took up positions either
side of me. "Dove's coming with us as he's never really integrated
into the camp. He needs to be somewhere he can be himself, to
practice his religion and be accepted as the priest he is. He's never
agreed to fight and kill, and that's okay with me. I'm coming with
you, not because the commandant wants me to squeeze you for
information or keep tabs on you, but because I discovered today, I
don't want to stay there. Not somewhere they think you're replace-
able or useful for the time being, then throw you aside."

J's caustic words surprised me. "But you're the team leader and
effectively moving up the ladder toward promotion. Or so I
thought."

Her smile wasn't sunny or happy. Instead, it was laced with self-
deprecation. "I'd talked myself into believing they saw me as part of
the whole. You know, big picture view. An important aspect of the
overall team. Clearly, that's not the case."

The need to tell her she was important hit hard, but I fought it
back. She didn't need me to tell her that. Besides, I doubted she
wanted my opinion.

Julia

Why did I tell him all this stuff? Dove touched my shoulder, and I grabbed his fingers, thanking him without words for the support he gave just by being there. He knew what I meant when I'd answered Leroy's question of why we were on the bus. He alone understood the ramifications of what had passed. I wanted Leroy to see just how deep this hurt went. Conversely, I also didn't want to tell Leroy exactly what the commandant had suggested so damned carefully. I was worth more than they gave me credit for, I told myself.

It didn't stop the hurt or sense of violation though.

But now I focused on what lay ahead. "I'm going to ask Liam and Elaine for a spot for all three of us at their camp. You said they'd offered you a role, and I'm sure both Dove and I will be of value to them too."

Leroy didn't answer, though his gaze narrowed. We remained companionable but silent for the rest of the trip. At the large metal gates, the bus pulled up and waited for them to open and admit us. Once within they shut with a clang, and the men cheered.

It was odd that they reacted like that, as if they'd returned home. *Home.* Such a small word but encapsulating so many emotions.

We stepped off the bus as Liam strode up. "Uh, Leroy, Dove, and Julia. What's going on?" His gaze bobbed between the three of us, and I stepped up.

"Leroy is planning on accepting your offer. I'm hoping you also have a space for Dove and me. Dove is a medic and priest, but the—"

Liam held up his hands. "Woah. How about we take this over to my office." He smiled at the men who'd returned. "Well done, everyone. Could you grab their bags and deliver them to my office? I'll take these three and see what's what."

"Sure" and "okay" floated over me.

I hadn't seen this aspect of the setup before but felt amazed at the way they responded to his requests for assistance. That he'd started out by letting them know they were valued made me feel good about my decision to be here.

"You've got a pretty tight ship here, yet you don't have the military carry-on happening."

"No, Julia. We've found that as a collective, we achieve more, and the group values the way we run the camp. Everyone is equal. The old have tasks, as do the young, and they're— we're—all contributing to the greater outcome."

I followed in silence now, watching as he chatted with one person, then inspected something else on the way to the house where he and his wife had set up the offices.

We stepped inside, and he gestured to the comfortable lounge chairs, indicating for us to sit, which we did. "So, tell me what brought you back."

Straight to the point. Great. *Not.* "Look, at the camp I felt that I was only there for one reason—to go out and kill zombies. When I questioned a directive, I was told that there may not be a place for me anymore. I'm not expendable though. I'm a human, and I need to be treated like someone who's valued. So, when the opportunity came, I took it."

Oh my God! Did I actually tell him all that? The verbal diarrhea exposed my underbelly and was something I'd fought really hard to overcome since the virus had hit.

Liam sat down, taking the seat before me, and I felt the probing gaze settling on me. "I see. We're always looking for people who have something to contribute. What were you before the virus?"

"I was second-in-command at the Registry of Births, Deaths, and Marriages."

I heard Leroy and Liam's indrawn breath then the bark of laughter from Dove. "Oh, that's amazing. All this time and I never knew that about you."

"Well, it's not really useful in a zombie apocalypse, now is it? I mean, have you ever gone up to a zombie and said, 'excuse me, what is your name and date of birth before I wipe you out'?"

Liam grinned. "Maybe not. But it's something we should re-institute. After all, we could all benefit from keeping records for those who come after us, once we beat this bloody thing. Plus, I take it you're a crack shot?"

I shrugged. "I used to shoot competitively before the virus. So, when I got stuck at the hospital, they made use of my skills."

"Welcome to our camp, Julia. I know you'll be an asset."

The meeting wore on for at least another hour, and when we were released exhaustion lay heavily on me.

"Find your way over to the hospital wing, Jeremy will help you," Liam said, and a young boy nodded from where he'd been waiting by the door. "And we'll get you officially into our systems." Liam shut the door, and the three of us followed the child to the house they'd converted into the surgery.

We entered the house.

"You need to talk with Ramon," Jeremy told us. "He's Liam's brother and a doctor. He'll take a few blood tests first, then you'll be given a medical."

The door opened and a big man entered what they'd turned into a waiting room. "Newcomers, hmm? Jeremy, take this back to Liam, if you wouldn't mind, and tell him I want to see Elaine today about four o'clock."

Jeremy's face screwed up. "She's not sick, is she?"

Ramon ruffled the boy's head. "No. Just a routine thing."

The boy took off, and Ramon grabbed some clipboards off the wall and passed them around.

"Fill these out first, then I'll come get you one by one. A medical and blood tests, plus some history. Makes it easier down the track if we need to give first aid."

It was like a *Twilight Zone* episode, I thought. You could have sent me to a doctor's surgery before the virus and I wouldn't have batted an eyelash. "Then what?" I enquired.

"I normally prescribe isolation, but since you were here yesterday, or the day before, if you have anything communicable, I reckon we would have seen evidence by now. So, we'll find you some temporary accommodation and go from there."

I plopped down into one of the seats and made my way through the questions, surprised that I was the first to rise and knock on the door as instructed.

Ramon, the doctor, smiled at me with kindness in his eyes and ushered me into the room. It had all the trappings of a proper surgery suite, amazing me, and I got through the routine of questions, including the ones about possible pregnancy, pap smears, and even contraceptive medication.

He shooed me out, and I waited as first Dove then Leroy entered the suite to return a little while later after their consultations as the door rattled and two women entered.

"Okay, here comes Elaine and Mrs. Garmin. They'll know where you're being housed," Ramon said.

Elaine smiled, her eyes shining. "Ramon, I got your message. I'm free now if that works." When she turned to us, the smile grew broader. "You're going to stay in the house next door. We've set it up as temporary accommodation for new camp members, and two of the three bedrooms have been set aside for you. Your bags have already been delivered there. Mrs. Garmin will show you where it is."

Once again, we found ourselves ushered onward into a house we hadn't entered before. The eighties décor was overwhelmed by a massive plasma screen on one wall and a floor-to- ceiling unit full of DVDs. I'll have to check this room out further, I told myself then followed Mrs. Garmin into a bedroom complete with its own en-suite.

"Now, dear, I thought this would be fine for you. The gentlemen can share the next room over and the bathroom down the hall. A woman needs her own toilet, you know."

Twilight Zone again, I thought but smiled.

She opened the wardrobe. "There's a choice of clothing, so grab what you need. Underwear in the chest of drawers, all new, and there's more where that came from."

I couldn't help gaping. "What did you do, empty a department store?"

"Well, we needed it, and with so many to clothe, feed, and house it seemed only right."

That shut me up.

Chapter 7

Leroy

WE'D BEEN HERE over a week, and thus far I hadn't yet met those I was supposed to tutor. We'd had a guided tour of the farm, the workshop where equipment was being made to assist in production of essential items, and even the stores.

"You'll need to apprise yourself of where everything is, as we roster everyone into a range of roles, but they won't be onerous, and since you're here to fulfill a special need, Leroy, that will be your first priority."

Elaine's voice droned on, talking about the system for bartering and acquisition of goods, but I watched as J walked slowly, hands in her pocket. The longer she was here, the calmer she'd become. Also, the closer she and Dove were.

Last night, I'd caught them deep in conversation on the front steps of the house. It wasn't like they were in a clinch, but the memory of seeing the closeness between them ate at me.

"Ramon has informed me he has all your medical history and test results. We'll be arranging your long-term accommodation. Dove—that name is your preference, yes?"

Dove nodded in agreement.

"You'll be given a separate, though small accommodation. You'll be able to set up a chapel, and if you're missing anything you need, let us know. We can make arrangements in the next scouting mission to secure the items. Although, with your permission we'd include you and of course Julia. Do you prefer J, because I noticed that's how most of the crew with you last time addressed you?"

J sidestepped and crashed into me. I steadied her with both hands. "Thanks," she croaked then shrugged away. "Um, J is fine, but my name is Julia. I think it was shortened just to make things easy at the beginning."

Elaine frowned. "Yes, so either J or Julia. We don't have any Julias, but we've got a Jeremy and Justine..."

We kept moving on, and I wondered just how much of herself J had boxed away in the long months since the virus hit. I wondered what she thought of me now... I stomped hard on those thoughts. "Uh, Elaine? When do you think we'll be able to, you know, do whatever roles you have planned?"

The woman turned. "Oh, tomorrow is fine. I've arranged an office space for Julia, and Liam has cleared a section of the camp for you. You'll meet your students tomorrow. I have your list of requirements here." She rustled through a file, and I wondered how the hell for all we'd changed, we still had to have paperwork. "Now, let's show you the permanent accommodation we've organized."

Julia
0800

It felt odd hearing my name in full again. After so many months, I'd become J, and dropping back into the other persona was uncomfortable. At least they'd understood that after so long on my own, being housed with my mother wasn't going to work for me. Not that I'd seen her since returning, but no doubt I would soon.

I was in the singles accommodation; an old unit block they'd annexed recently. "The camp seems to keep growing, so we looked around, planned how we could access what we needed. The fencing here is strong enough, but Liam said it's pretty much the furthest section we could reinforce with what we've scavenged. He's thinking about satellite communities soon," Elaine had told me, and I had nodded.

Grow too fast and they couldn't put in the time to ensure the safety of those living within the confines. Their thought patterns were sensible and well-considered.

The clothes I'd taken from the cupboard and the others I'd requisitioned were sitting in the cupboard of the unit that was now mine, and I sighed. It wasn't a lot, but it would do. Rations were to be collected daily and cooked in the shared kitchen zone, and each unit was broken into two with the old kitchens renovated to bathrooms so that the singles zone comprised of a hallway leading to bedroom and bathroom, the rest excised off into another small unit and a tiny kitchenette for making coffee and tea.

Just this morning I'd woken for the first time in what was my own space. It felt right.

I hurried to the bathroom, washed my face and brushed my teeth, then returned to the bedroom, sliding into gloriously clean clothes, new ones I hadn't stained or worn out. The shoes were a tight fit but slip-ons. I'd missed that comfort having lived in combat boots for the duration.

With a nod at myself in the tiny mirror, I scurried out of my unit. The keys in my pocket reminded me that human nature was a strange thing, and I locked the door before heading out.

The fresh air felt untainted as it washed over my face on the way to the old school, where Elaine had set up my office.

The first job was to take stock of the people in the camp. Ages and so on. A kind of census she'd said, and I agreed it was important. Where at the beginning it had been taking names and skills when they arrived, with the camp growing some things had slid, according to Liam. Then they'd explained the reason Elaine was keen to hand over the role. "I'm pregnant," she'd shared, and I couldn't help but think that this would be the luckiest of babies born into a new, if exceptionally dangerous, world.

The computer they'd found for me sat on the desk, but I ignored it for now, settling in with a notepad and pen.

How long I'd been working when the rap on the door caught my attention I couldn't say. Leroy stepped inside and dropped into the seat opposite me. "You didn't make lunch in the eatery. I've brought you something."

The stew smelled appetizing, and my stomach rumbled, reminding me I'd skipped breakfast too. "I got sidetracked." I indicated to the piles of files I'd created on the table behind me.

"Even you need to eat." He pushed the bowl in my direction. "You've done a lot," he said as I made my way through the bowl and the thick hunk of bread.

"Yeah, well, I agree a census is the first step, then I can create records for every member born, died, or married here. Track where they came from and so on."

"So you can report it back to the commandant?"

My gut lurched, but I shook my head with slow moves. "No. But I do think it will help us pinpoint what might be a factor in the speed of their transition, variabilities and so on. For the sake of finding a vaccine or cure. I know Ramon was working on one, but it didn't pan out. The culture didn't survive the zombie virus, he said. The serums we brought in were also damaged during shipment. Likely that mad run across the alley."

"And you blame me." His face shuttered.

I started at Leroy's words. "No! No, I don't."

"But since I told you, you've kept your distance."

I chewed my lip. "It's not so much that I don't want to be with you or blame you. I was surprised, I admit, but it didn't occur to me that our government or parts of it would be behind such a heinous act. You were acting under orders. That's what soldiers do, right?"

He nodded, and I scanned his face. "But you didn't want me to touch you."

I laughed at that for just a moment, but the import of his reaction sobered me. Reaching out, I touched his hand. "Oh God, no. I want you so much, but since the virus I haven't really connected with anyone. You scare me, Damien Leroy. Far too much for comfort."

"And Dove?"

Ahhh. He'd been cool toward me since the night he'd caught us out on the porch talking. "Is a friend. A good friend, but there'll never be more than that. He and I were discussing the world and our place. What we wanted. Stuff like that," I said, hoping he'd stop asking. In truth, I'd been talking to Dove about him. Explaining the confusion of emotions I didn't seem able to untangle.

"Okay. So, I'm supposed to help you in the afternoons. I get three hours in the morning with my crew then some other light duties later in the afternoon, but I'm yours between one and three. What do you want me to do?"

I blinked slowly. *Strip me naked, kiss every inch of skin...* Hold it right there, I told my brain. I'd wager that wasn't what Elaine had planned.

"Um, I'm going to start creating the questionnaires. Once they're printed, I need copies made. Could you do that?"

He pointed at the printer plugged into the corner. "Is that a set-and-forget model?"

I laughed. "Yeah, I think so. Let me write this up, then we can see together."

Leroy

Working mornings with the fifteen kids wasn't easy. They were aged between seven and twelve, so their physical fitness was as varied as their education. I needed to remember that and start slow.

A couple were trained in martial arts or had at least the rudimentary knowledge. It would have been great if we'd been fighting ninjas, I guessed, having watched the way they threw themselves at their assigned tasks *á la* Bruce Lee.

Still, I talked to them about building themselves up, including a regime of lifting weights, food choices, and running to increase their stamina. Together, we trained in forms of hand-to- hand and also brainstormed ways to find weapons in a surprise attack. Interestingly enough, they formed a strong team, buddying up without direction so the strongest was there to assist the weakest member of their team.

They weren't ready for more, and certainly not for leaving the camp. They weren't ready to tackle zombies yet, except perhaps for those missing all their limbs, and even then, that was questionable at best.

They weren't exactly impressed with my plans, but I'd continue down this path, because training them carefully meant when the skills were needed, they'd be second nature, and hopefully they'd be a cohesive unit.

The early afternoons were spent with Julia, as she now called herself—though I tended to still call her J, as did Dove—creating the documents and arranging timetables to meet with every person in the camp to collect the data necessary.

"So, what will you do with this information?" I asked.

"We'll keep an accurate account of everyone who comes in and out, be able to update births, deaths, marriages, and so on. It will come into its own, trust me, especially when it comes time to remember those we've lost."

"Is that why you ask if they've had children or do have?"

Julia nodded. "We know that in some cases whole families disappeared. In others, family members lost track of each other, and perhaps down the line, we'll be able to share what we know and reunite families."

Late afternoons were different. I'd been co-opted to help care for the animals. None of it was exactly hard work, with fetching water, collecting eggs, or even milking some cows. Everything was being done the old-fashioned way, but it felt good.

The small phone beside Julia squawked, and she picked it up as if it were a dangerous snake. "Uh, hello?"

Her countenance changed and tightened, cheeks flaming bright red, and her fingers wound tight around the receiver. So tight the

knuckles of her fingers turned white. "No, sir. I'm not going to—
No!" She slammed the receiver down as fury flared in her eyes.
"Conceited bastard!" she yelled, and both her hands flew up,
covering her face.

"What?" I demanded, but she shook her head.

Unable to prevent it, I reached out, took her wrists in my hand,
and pulled. Her eyes now resembled pools of anguish. "I can't tell
you, Leroy," she sniffed. "I mean I feel so damned dirty."

"The commandant?" It was a guess, but of the educated variety,
that she answered with a nod. "He wanted information?" I
suggested, and she nodded again. "On me and what I know?"

"Yeah."

I knew instantly what he'd asked her to do. All it took was a look
at the way she slumped and tugged away from my touch.

I inhaled deeply then simply blurted it out. "He wants you to
sleep with me for the information."

Julia reared back, answering my question.

"Fucking bastard," I ground out. "I'll tell you anything when
you ask, if I can answer. But not like that. You don't need to..."

Now she dropped her face to her hands and cried in silence.
The way her body shuddered cracked my heart in two. I damned
the commandant and Allan to hell for their careless and
demeaning handling of a strong woman. They'd stripped her
naked with their crude demands, reducing her to a messy lump of
human misery.

"I know you wouldn't do that, Julia."

"But that's..." She stumbled, cleared her throat, and tried again.
"He asked me before I came here, Leroy. It's why I left Queanbeyan. I couldn't stay once he'd made that suggestion. When I said
no, he said there'd probably be no place for me there." Her voice
quavered, and I had to curl my hands into tight fists as bursts of
energy zipped through my nervous system.

"You tell me what he wants to know, baby, and I'll help if I can,"
I crooned, hyperaware that she needed to be treated with gentleness
and respect right now.

She sniffed. "I didn't wait to hear."

I grinned, because she hadn't lost her spine even though he'd treated her with obvious contempt. "Atta girl."

She scrubbed at her face. "That's easy for you to say. You drift here and there without ties or friends."

Her words sobered me. "Yes and no. I do that because of the mistakes I made. Because I'm a coward, J." I knew it was the truth now; a realization I'd made with shame attached.

Now she tugged on my hands. "Still. Maybe that's what I should do."

I shook my head, well aware that in no way would she feel better about being a drifter. "No, J. You're reliable and—"

Her bitter laugh stopped me. "Don't think I'm some kind of hero. I'm not. I just made the best of a bad situation. In the end, leaving Queanbeyan behind was easier than I expected. I just..." I heard her breathe heavily. "I just left."

For a moment I considered her words. I could take them at face value, but I wouldn't. I knew this woman now and understood the hurt which drove her away from the relative safety she'd inhabited.

"Leroy?"

"Yeah, J?"

"I could go with you."

Oh my God! The words hit hard, like a sucker punch in the gut. I wanted her to. I wanted to have sex with her, it was true, and to keep her close. My body ached for her day and night. Still, a seed of honesty forced me to shake my head. "No, J. Because you're a believer. A member of a family and a team player. I'm not."

"Bullshit. If you weren't, you wouldn't be helping the kids. They rely on you to be there for them. You set that up. You taught them you were their leader. You're the biggest team player I know."

Nausea threatened to swamp me, because I knew she was right. Somehow, and at some time, I'd become one of the crew again. A leader and a follower. It filled the holes I'd attempted to ignore deep inside me.

Pushing up from the chair and away didn't stop the truth. Couldn't make it easier to hear, because the last time I'd been that,

I'd failed. I'd been instrumental in the death of millions. All because I'd made poor choices.

"No, J. I'm not." There was a hoarse edge to my voice, and I couldn't disguise the way my body betrayed the fear that welled deep in the pit of my belly.

"Leroy?" She shoved away from her chair, arms twining around me. "What's wrong?"

I shook my head as the sudden sensation of regret and guilt swamped me. "I caused this." Her fingers dug into my back and worried me like a ragdoll.

"No. They would have done it anyway, whether you were involved or not. And it's not like you could have said no, right? I mean, you were recruited to that team for a reason. They needed you and your skills. They didn't tell you everything before the mission, you were just sent out there without all the knowledge to do their work."

The lump wedged in my chest shrank a little. "I just... I hate knowing that I played a part in this."

"It's okay to feel sad and awful. You just have to find a way forward though. To meet every day with the best of intentions and leave the world better when you're done."

There lay the crux of the matter. Leave it better. *If only.*

Chapter 8

Julia

MY SHIFT ENDED with me helping in the community gardens. I'd never really had the opportunity to get my hands in the dirt. Before everything happened, I lived in a high-rise apartment, and my mum had been the gardener when I lived at home—always her domain. It felt good and right to sink my fingers into the soil, though I needed a lot of assistance.

Elaine dropped down beside me. "You need to pull these ones. They're weeds." Her deft movements were hypnotic, and I watched then followed her lead.

"I rather like this."

She laughed. "My grandmother, who left me the cottage, taught me a lot about gardening. She always said that having blooming things around her lifted her spirits. And speaking of spirits..." She rocked back on her heels. "The commandant contacted Liam. Said you'd been insubordinate. Want to tell me about that?"

I groaned and noted for the first time that everyone else in the patch had left. "I, um... He wanted me to get information for him. To sleep with Leroy to obtain it and report back. I refused."

She didn't betray any shock, and her hand slid over mine, relieving me of some of the fears that gnawed at me. "Some people will never understand that leadership isn't about issuing orders that make their subordinates feel dirty. Our camp doesn't work like that, so while I'll talk with Liam, I know he'll agree that you've done nothing wrong. You don't need to use sex to gain information or favor here. However, I have to ask, what information was he particularly after?"

This was tricky ground. I didn't know what Leroy had told them specifically, and I felt it wrong to share such intelligence. "I think it would be best if I asked Leroy to tell you."

She nodded. "About the mission he was sent on? The inoculation of the water system?" I nodded, even more discomforted.

"That's okay. Leroy and Liam have discussed it. The scientists who went with you to Queanbeyan clued Ramon in on most of their findings before they left. They also indicated they'd heard of zombies who were more evolved."

My gut clenched. "Evolved? Like how?"

Elaine shook her head. "They heard they were communicating. In a rudimentary way, but nonetheless working together."

If they worked together, it meant nothing good for humanity. I rubbed my brow. "What about—"

"I don't know any more. Just that Ramon heard the information and has been spending more hours than ever in the laboratory we put together for him. He's working now on a vaccine so no one else becomes a zombie. But when he heard about this, he said we need some tissue samples to chart any changes in the virus. Mutations. We're going to need some samples of the evolved zombies, and Liam hoped you and Leroy would join the team. We need reliable people who know what they're doing, and you both seem to be quite skilled."

My breath caught in my throat. For a non-militaristic camp what they were asking was...odd. "I don't want to kill anymore, Elaine."

Elaine laid a soft hand on mine. "We understand that. We're hoping you'll be able to bring us some fresh specimens without needing to harvest from the zombies. Intelligence from south of here says that with the initial frenzy and glut of fresh humans over, they turned on each other. They've changed again since then, we think, as the communication grows more effective. You saw that with the incident I believe? The ones involving the dogs. They hunt in packs, because it means they have a greater chance of success. We need to know what changes have taken place in their DNA. What has caused the changes from sentient and thinking humans to ravening beasts who crave the flesh of the living. Ramon said he's not sure there is a single strain because of the way the initial virus was spread and individualized evolutions, so we need to know more before we can create an effective vaccine. We need to be sure of just how many strains there are. We can only do that by getting our hands on fresh samples, Julia."

What she asked was both simple and yet also difficult. I wanted to help, but I'd laid down my rifle, found peace, and could once again sleep at night without the constant wearing dreams. If I stepped back into that world, would I lose the last remaining remnants of myself?

Yet, what they asked was small, and they asked instead of ordering.

Confusion warred, but she needed an answer. I inhaled, the rich, earthy scent filling my senses. They'd given me this and so much more. A sense of belonging. Of being useful. Time to take a chance, I thought. "Yes."

Elaine gazed into my eyes. "You don't have to."

"I know." I honestly did, and that settled the nerves that jumped in my belly.

"All right then. I'll let Liam and Leroy know. By the way, Liam is calling a meeting of the single members tomorrow morning at eight AM. He'll come to your complex."

With so much to consider I didn't ask why, simply returned to my task.

We worked in silence for a while, until Elaine levered herself up. "I think that's sufficient for today."

I made my way back to the small apartment now I called home.

For the first time since this contagion had been released, I sought silence and something more.

Inside the rooms, I headed for the shower, shucked off my clothes, and stepped within the cubicle, welcoming the water that washed over me. Metaphorically, it was like being reborn, but while it made me feel more comfortable it didn't quell the sudden emptiness I needed to fill.

I toweled with quick movements and headed for the bedroom beyond and slid into clean clothing. Scraping back my hair into a careless ponytail, I caught sight of myself in the mirror.

The gaunt look I'd sported weeks ago had disappeared in the scant month I'd been here. No streaks of gray that many had gained since the outbreak marred my hair. It was as if I'd been 'untouched', but I knew better.

"At least I lost all those extra pounds I was carrying before the virus," I muttered, surveying my flat stomach.

Sliding into the shoes, I left my apartment and hurried down below.

Already a group from our block had gathered, and the scent of cooking meat wafted as did something else I hadn't smelled in a long time.

"Who found wine?" I couldn't suppress the squeak of surprise.

"We were saving it for a rainy day. That's today," called a woman seated at the table.

I must have screwed up my nose, because suddenly Leroy was there, running his finger down it.

"What?" I demanded.

"We've survived a year since the first known outbreak was televised," Leroy whispered.

I gaped at him and turned blindly to the others gathered. "Really?"

"May fourth was the day it was first detected, and the indicators televised. On the fifth, the airports were shut down."

The chill in the air nipped at me, and I turned back to Leroy. "Wow. Today is the fourth of May?"

He nodded. "Yep, has been all day. Didn't you see on your computer monitor?"

I shook my head and jerked back when something touched my hand. I was being handed a glass of wine. I accepted it with shaking fingers.

"We're celebrating. We've survived the first year, and David had some wine stashed, which he shared. Next year it'll be strictly home brew unless we find an abandoned bottle shop."

The ridiculousness of that comment made me laugh. "Fair enough," I sputtered once the outburst passed.

We raised a glass and toasted our survival before the meal was served, then enjoyed several more glasses after.

Leroy

Julia relaxed with several glasses of wine under her belt. Hell, we all did, but watching her ditch her inhibitions was...*amazing*. It was as if a switch had been flicked and the woman from before made her entrance. She was witty and engaging, unlike the cold and unresponsive woman I'd met weeks before in Queanbeyan.

Unable to help myself, I gravitated to her side and stayed within touching distance as if some invisible string held us together.

"I never really wanted to stay in an office environment, but it's all I know, or knew," she rattled on, taking hold of my hand.

I gripped it tight as she wobbled uncertainly. "But you're really good at what you do."

The smile she turned in my direction warmed me inside, turning me mushy and gooey. "Thank you, Leroy. But can I call you Damien? I mean, since we're here now." She waved her arm and her entire body followed it.

"Sure, Julia."

"I used to shoot when I was younger. Well, bow and arrows anyway. Won a few prizes."

"Ahh. No wonder you're quick. You would have been good at it."

She shrugged, and I grinned.

Her smile lit up my insides so they melted just a little further.

The first members of our group, somewhat intoxicated but also quite happy, drifted off; some as couples and others by themselves. I was struck dumb with the thought that maybe, if I asked, she'd allow me to kiss her. "Julia?"

She blinked solemnly. "Yes?"

"Can I kiss you?"

The grin on her face widened. "It's taken you a long time to ask." She reached up and gripped the sleeves of my t-shirt. "Come on then."

Her tug pulled me forward, and our lips met with a smack while my brain exploded at the sensation of her body against mine. The scent of her filled my nostrils, the aroma enticingly musky. The fog in my brain grew just like this hunger for Julia.

It was difficult to keep my brain working on any kind of level. Sanity blurred the edges of fantasy, but I pulled away. "Julia," I groaned. "We've been drinking. I don't know about you, but my head is pretty damned fuzzy." I didn't want her to think back on tonight and say I'd taken advantage. Besides, so much wasn't yet clear to me.

Instead of drawing away, her grin turned hot. "Perhaps, but I don't care. Please, Damien, tonight, be with me."

Oh. My. God. It was the first time she'd used my given name like that, and the way she whispered it against my lips made it the strongest aphrodisiac ever.

"Julia..."

Her finger slipped over my lips. "Shhh, just feel."

Boy, could I feel her, the way she undulated against me, a houri in the dimness.

"Come with me, Damien. Come to my bed."

I swallowed the lump that had settled in my throat. I wanted her so badly my entire groin burned, my brain swam, and the frantic beating of my heart surely had to be audible to her.

As her warm breath caressed my skin, I caved. "Yes," I hissed and allowed her to lead me toward the steps. When we reached her apartment, I stopped. "Julia?"

"Brushing me off?" For all her bravado, I heard the seed of uncertainty, and it crushed any lingering resistance. Instead, I swooped in, wordlessly reminding her that I desired her. Her alone.

The tangle of our mouths and tongues fanned the flames inside my belly. The fog of hunger crept further into my senses, and now I wanted more. I wanted her. Skin to skin. I wanted it now.

We turned the handle and stumbled inside, my hands already under the cotton of her shirt, sliding over miles of silken skin. Her breath caught as she tugged away, just enough to close the door and begin the process of unbuttoning. The madness of need tempered with the knowledge that everything was too hard to come by had me tugging my shirt over my head.

The lights flickered, but her eyes shone. Her mouth, raspberry ripe, opened a little as she panted for breath.

I dug deep into my pants, withdrew the two small foil packets, and held them up. "Just in case."

Her throaty laugh tantalized my senses, and I pulled at the tongue of my belt, flicked the metal spike from the hole so the ends swung free, then started on the button and zipper of my jeans. I felt them drop to the floor then promptly forgot about them because my vision was filled with the view of a goddess.

White bra and panties and nothing else but smooth, delectable skin. My hand shook as I reached out, and she whispered, "I want you, Damien Leroy."

My brain blanked out, leaving me reacting on autopilot.

Julia

The alcoholic fog fled as I stood before him in just my underwear. It wasn't pretty or anything special, though it was comfortable —usually—but tonight I really wished it were silk and lace.

Even with the unassuming cloth covering me, it was the look on his face, the shine in his eyes, and the way his chest moved that told me he wanted me. Who I was here and now.

His look fed a hunger I didn't even know existed inside me. When he reached out, his hand shook, and I hoped it was with the same hunger that welled inside me. I stepped forward. Desperation and need growing and making it hard to breathe. Heat suffused every part of my body, and longing throbbed between my legs. In my mind, the next move took on that of a precipice, but brushing aside my fear of rejection, I reached back, unclipped my bra, and shrugged it off.

He moaned, and I couldn't help the smile that slid over my face. "Like what you see?"

"Oh God, yes," he groaned, and he closed the gap between us, reaching around me with one arm so our bodies collided.

The rasp of the lightly haired skin of his chest brushing against my nipples sent ripples of hunger coursing through my veins.

"Come with me," I whispered, and we slowly moved together toward the bed. It creaked as we dropped, and I couldn't help the laugh. "Good thing there's no one else here."

He slid the foil packets onto the bedside table then returned all his attention to me. His gaze zeroed in on my mouth, and my lips parted as he dipped toward me. Skin to skin, breath to breath, and mouth to mouth we moved, his hands at my waist, brushing away the panties as I followed his lead, sliding my fingers beneath the layers of cotton to find the firm globes of his ass.

His fingertips roamed over newly naked flesh, and I moved, squirmed, and whispered of my need. "Touch me, Leroy."

"Thought I was Damien?" he purred.

"You are, but right now, I can barely think."

Leroy laughed, just a tiny sound, then his features changed again. "So beautiful," he whispered against the sensitive flesh of my neck.

I arched, needing more while the burn grew. Emptiness, the sort I'd never known, had filled me up, and I needed him to fix it. I wanted and hungered. Yearned for the fulfilment I knew instinctively only he could give me.

We moved together, flesh to flesh. "You're naked," I wheezed, and he laughed, the rumble a shockwave on my now beleaguered senses.

He pulled back, and I got my first look at him. An Adonis in the darkness. A boom of thunder impinged, and I swallowed. "A storm coming."

"It's fitting, don't you think?"

Oh yeah. "Come back to me."

"In a moment." He grabbed one of the foil packs, and I watched him tear it open and apply the condom. He hadn't asked and I didn't have to request, and in that moment something clicked.

I shied away from deep thought and welcomed him back to my arms. We clung then, lips and fingers questing, sighs echoing in the quiet until finally, achingly, he settled himself between my legs.

"Open for me, beautiful."

I did. His cock, hard and ready, nudged at my center. His fingers traced the lips of my aching pussy, sliding over the pearl he'd uncovered as I cried out, longing and hunger biting at me.

"Please," I called, but he simply continued the assault. Every glance shattering my restraint as my fingers wound into the bedding.

"So damned beautiful," he crooned with guttural tones, before sliding a single digit deep inside me. "So hot and ready. Wet. Will I fit?"

I rolled my hips, wanting this and more. "I want you." And unable to wait further, I grasped his hand, the finger he'd buried sliding from inside me, and I mewled. "Inside me. *Please.*"

Winding my legs around his lean waist, I tugged him closer and slid his hands over my aching breasts. With a tight laugh, he moved, inched himself once more to my very center and slid deeply within my body.

Stretched. Filled. Then he shifted, nudged, and I cried out. The wild dance began to its own erotic rhythm. One that sped up quickly while the tension inside me mounted. Crested. Then I shattered in his arms, my entire body slumping down with a strange mix of exhaustion and repletion.

I felt him slide again and again, arching and grunting until he stiffened, groaned, and finally slid bonelessly against me, his weight a heavy blanket.

A moment of clarity impinged. Either I'd made the best decision of my life or the worst. Which one remained to be seen.

Chapter 9

Leroy

Waking was disconcerting. I was warm, arms wound around me, and for a moment the past overlaid the here and now. I almost called Katrina's name, but the fingers that lay against my chest weren't long claws of some opalescent sheen. The wisps of hair on my chest weren't blonde.

Reality hit like a sledgehammer, and heaven knows the stutter of my heart certainly wasn't easy to explain.

Memories of the plague-infested zombies, the images of undead, and the remembered blows and scraping fingers couldn't be willed away. But I was warm and comfortable. My mind clear for the first time with plans of what I wanted for my future...I wanted Julia. I wanted the chance at a forever.

I turned and met her gaze, surprised to discover that she'd been awake the whole time I'd been grappling with my thoughts and memories.

Her fingers wound into the chain around my neck. "Tell me about her."

I closed my eyes. "Katrina. We'd only been engaged a few

weeks when I was sent out to inoculate the water system. She promised to wait until I was back before we made it public. I got back and she was..." The bubble of pain I'd worn like a cape seemed not so overwhelming now. "I found her at the unit. Did the best I could by her. Took the ring to remember her by and kept going."

"What was she like?"

I laughed. "A beautician. So the hair, nails, and makeup were key. She used to complain I should wax and use product. We met when I was in the Northern Territory. I was stationed at Larrakeyah Barracks, and she was second-in-command at the local salon. We were going hot and strong for a year or so, then I was reassigned. She moved with me when I was stationed at Lavarack. She loved the lifestyle. The beach and community."

"Did you still love her?" Shock erupted on her face. "Ohmygod. I take that back. I shouldn't have asked."

I reached over and touched her hand. "No, it's okay. I thought I did at the time. I mean, we had history and plans. But now I don't know."

Julia was strangely silent now.

I slipped my hand around hers, which was still tangled in the chain around my neck. "I can take this off."

Her eyes were watery as she met my gaze. "No. You need to wear it in memory of her."

There were undertones of pain and something else in her voice, and my stomach clenched hard. "What's wrong?"

She shook her head and simply pulled away.

The loss of her beside me overwhelmed. "Julia, talk to me."

She smiled, but I knew it was pasted on for my benefit. "Come on. We need to get moving. Liam wanted to meet with all of us downstairs by eight."

"So I heard. Know what it's about?"

She evaded my gaze and shook her head. "No."

The confusion I seemed to deal with daily settled in again, and I sighed. "Did I say something wrong?"

The look she gave me told me without words to 'shut up', and being no one's fool, that's exactly what I did. It didn't mean that I wouldn't toss it over in my mind though.

The others assembled downstairs, some decidedly disheveled and others hung over. A couple of them quirked an eyebrow at seeing the two of us together, and I couldn't help the seed of warmth in my belly at that.

Liam welcomed me by his side, and I took the seat, even though my attention centered on Julia.

"Welcome to everyone. Today I need to talk to you about something that is vitally important to the running of this compound. Children."

That caught my attention, and I swiveled, wondering if it had something to do with my charges.

"As you know, we're now twelve months on from the initial reports of the outbreak. At this point, we move from simply sustaining life to ensuring the survival of our people. Our interaction with the outside world is limited. With the communications systems down, it's not like we can simply pick up the phone and dial. My contact with other camps leads me to believe that some limited communication is going on between members of the government and overseas governments, but the civilians who have not succumbed do not have the knowledge to hack into the systems that remain. So, while some nine children have been born in this compound in the last twelve months, most were conceived pre-outbreak. Right now, that's not such an issue with thirty-two aged between birth and fifteen, however, it simply won't represent enough to sustain us as we age. And this is where this conversation gets tricky. We know of other encampments throughout Australia. Some will thrive with youngsters, but others won't. We need to plan for the future now. What we're asking is you consider partnering up to produce a replacement for yourself. We don't need you all to do so immediately, but this is something that needs to be addressed for the long-term viability of this community."

My gaze shot to Julia. I couldn't help it, because the sudden vision of her, naked, pregnant with my child, acted as a magnet. But it was the dawning horror on her face, the way her pupils dilated in shock as she looked back at me that pulled me up short.

She turned white, and for a moment I was sure she'd faint. Not the reaction a man expected, to be honest, when thinking about one's prospective partner carrying his child.

Julia

The words took me by surprise. A child. A replacement.

I was only twenty-three, and yet I'd done things with my life that just twelve months before would have seemed inconceivable. I'd gone from an office girl to warrior and back again. I'd met a man who made me burn, but also who'd given his heart to another, and now this.

I wanted to break away from the group, but others had crowded in behind me.

"What if I don't want to?" called the girl beside me, voicing what now stuck in my throat. *At least, not yet,* I should have added, but fear kept me silent.

"We can't make you at this point, but part of being a member of the compound means giving back. The truth is, without enough youngsters, eventually you will starve to death. Or not have carers, or any one of a range of things, including guards."

Liam's words shut her up along with the murmurs that had begun to sweep through the gathered crowd.

Leroy cleared his throat. "Not everyone should need to do that right now, and I'm sure arrangements can be made for those who don't wish to parent, am I right, Liam?"

"We can make those arrangements if necessary, but every fertile woman between the ages of eighteen and thirty-five will need to consider birthing at least one child in the coming couple of years. Unless something changes significantly, including our finding a way to communicate with the outside world and overcoming the zombie plague, which isn't looking so good right now. Given no country will have contact with us while this virus is raging, it's that or die out."

Here was ground I was comfortable with. Facts and information. "What about the serum?"

Liam glanced at me. "Failure on the first three batches created in the last month, which is why you've been requested to join the hunt for fresh specimens."

I nodded. I was useful on that front. And I turned away, ready to head for my office when Liam called my name.

"Julia, could you stay a moment please?"

Turning back, I noted that the others were melting away along with a fair bit of muttering. Many would be working in the fields, some were heading off to guard duty, and others to take up tasks necessary to the day-to-day running of the compound.

As the last person left, bar Liam and Leroy, I addressed Liam. "Yes?"

"We're going to need fresh specimens. Draw up a list of requirements, team members you think would be useful, and liaise with Leroy on a path you feel best suits our needs. You'll also take my brother Ramon with you."

"Is he any good in the field?"

Liam winced. "Not really. He's a doctor and immunologist. He'll be your scientific brains and will require a personal guard too. He's got skills we can't afford to lose, and he's my brother. We need you to move out as soon as possible, so get the information together as fast as you can."

I must have stood there like a fish out of water, gasping for breath when Liam took my hand. "This is important to our survival. If we can immunize against the plague, we can then focus on disposal."

"Uh, yeah, sure." There didn't seem to be much else to say.

With a single nod in Leroy's direction, Liam turned on his heel and left us.

Was this the new world I inhabited? The one where I had choices, but each more difficult and emotionally draining than the other? I couldn't stop the curl of my hand or the rapid beat of my heart. Leroy advanced, the sound of his footsteps crunching on the old concrete capturing my attention.

"I'm sorry. I can see how hard this is for you." He reached out, touched my hand, and I couldn't help but latch on and hold tight.

Leroy

The day passed slowly. The kids moved through their exercises and training sessions. Then I headed out into the fields to plow the ground that had been roads prior to the plague. It seemed that everything was returning to nature. I couldn't help but contemplate the fact that life had been this simple a hundred years or more ago.

Sure, there were zombies. We could see them through the perimeter fence, some with fingers curled into the wire, their faces slack, the moans low and at times even blood-curdling. Now and then one would push against the fence and the guards would deal with it, but for the most part we ignored them, safe within the enclave.

I tried to shove aside the situation with Julia, but my brain kept returning to it. Not my emotional attachment, because I'd already come to terms with that, but the problem of how she'd deal with the task we'd been set. Tonight we'd sit down and plan the mission, but I couldn't help but consider the emotional cost to her.

As dusk neared, we collected our equipment and made our way back to the buildings, passing the fresh guards who'd remain out there until around midnight. I scanned their faces, but for all the banter as they passed, they were just like the rest of us, folks doing a job. One that was distasteful, and from time to time exacting, but nonetheless, it was a part of the daily routine now.

I headed into my tiny apartment, showered, and returned to the downstairs communal kitchen area, and there she was, assisting with the preparation. Sidling up beside her, I sniffed the air. "What's cooking? Smells great."

"It's a lamb hot pot. We're going to try dehydrating the leftover ingredients so we can make meals on the road. We're almost out of the cache of MREs that were acquired last year, so I'm told."

Her answer had an odd, remote sound, and I looked at her, gazed into her eyes. She'd retreated back to the distanced J I'd met in Queanbeyan.

"Julia?"

"J," she corrected me absently while stirring the pot.

"Dammit, Julia," I began, but she cut me off.

"Planning is taking place here at eight. I've got the maps from Liam, the team lists I've managed to cobble together, and a resources list drawn up. It could be a long night." She peered into the pot. "This is done." She hauled the big pot up and over to the sink as I turned off the gas.

I sat beside her as we ate, stewing over the emotional distance she'd put between us. After the clearing up was finished she grabbed a box from the corner of the room and began setting up.

Every time I moved near her, hoping to talk privately, she'd stiffen up, so I waited, hoping for another opportunity. Liam, Ramon, and Dove trailed into the room and laid waste to any chance I had of sorting out the mess between us.

"You've been busy," Liam said as he looked over the piles of paper and maps.

"Better to have a good idea early on than make a huge mistake. I asked Dove along too, as I think he's got a better idea of the area than most of us. He was a local, as I understand it. Liam, I know you and Ramon weren't from around here. I was only here on holiday, so my knowledge is not so great and mainly of the Queanbeyan area, and Leroy is the same being fairly recent to the area."

Watching as she took control, it hit me that she was a natural leader. Her attention to detail, formulation of contingency plans, and so on reinforced this to me.

"This area here seems to be the biggest known congregation point of the evolving zombies according to your sources, Liam. We're best to avoid it and get to where it tapers off." Her finger pointed to an area, and Liam simply grunted. "We're going to have to take the long way around, but we can check out housing and structures. See if there is anything useful, and stockpile as we go. If it works to our advantage, we can return and collect the items at a later date."

"That'll slow you down," Liam said.

She glanced up at him. "Yes, but it's going to be slow anyway. I'd say at least a week or two, given we don't know what we're going to find and we're going to need to stay out of sight. However, it will give us valuable intel, and even better, we can look at increasing our supplies."

"All right. But we still need to decide on when."

Dove cleared his throat. "The weather is cooling. We don't want to leave it too long, otherwise we're going to be butting up against June and the really cold weather. It's bad enough now, but only going to get worse. While it rarely snows, the weather will drop to about two to four degrees Celsius overnight, making it close to freezing. We can't afford to be caught in that."

Liam scowled. "What are the chances that will kill off some of the zombies, Ramon?"

His brother shrugged. "We haven't done a lot of work on cold weather effects and the shufflers. I'll be able to gather anecdotal info though as it may assist in dealing with the ongoing issue, but we don't know the situation from last year because..."

Julia finished the thought, "Because we were all still in survival mode. You're right of course. This is the first opportunity we've had to get an up close and personal look and to gauge if it has any appreciable effect on their numbers. We just don't want to be so up close they can get to us."

No one laughed.

"I'm with Dove though," she continued. "We need to get out earlier rather than later. I think we could be ready to leave in say about forty-eight hours if we all pull together. Liam, I've taken the liberty of chatting with Elaine and drawing up a list of useful people. The team should be smaller, leaving less of a trail, so we need experienced personnel only. You want Ramon included, and we need Dove as a guide. Four guards for the team and Ramon's personal guard and Leroy as my offsider should be more than enough. Ramon, will you require cooling facilities for the specimens?"

"Yes, otherwise within a short period of time they won't be useable."

I watched as Julia gnawed on her thumbnail. "Do we have any of the snap-ice packs, Liam?"

He stared at her. "Snap-ice packs? What are they?"

Ramon started to laugh. "I like the way she thinks. Seriously though, the samples will have a limited life span at any temp we can carry them at. Even with those instant gel packs, we'll have to watch to make sure we keep them at between two and four degrees Celsius, and they'll only be good for about seven days. That means we'll need to get any medical researchers who may be alive here by the time we arrive back."

"You can't freeze them when you get back here?" Liam scratched his head.

The look Ramon speared at Liam almost made me laugh. But it wasn't really a laughing matter, so I smothered the sound before it escaped.

"No, brother. We'll have already compromised the samples. We'll need to get back here fast. Can we manage to do that within forty-eight hours, Julia?"

"Maybe. Depends on what we find, how much we can ditch in terms of weight, and the team," she answered.

"What about just using a vehicle?" asked Ramon.

Liam sighed. "There's more than one factor there. We're running low on fuel. We're going to send one vehicle out to collect the immunologists. It will speed up the process of getting them here to work on the samples, but we know that the zombies in that area scatter when they hear a vehicle. We'd have to chase the zombies into their lair to get what we need, and it's just too dangerous, so it makes more sense to send you further into the field."

I frowned. There were holes in that explanation I could drive a truck through, but I was also aware that now wasn't the time to mention them to Liam. I'd have to wait and see if there was more to this later on.

Chapter 10

Julia

IN THE WEEKS since I'd last pulled on a pack, I'd relaxed. Allowed life's pace to change for the better and had felt free and almost normal again. Today though, that sense of peace was tipped upside down. The weight of the bag on my back settled heavily on my shoulders, and the pistol in the holster at my side was bumped by the rifle slung carefully over my shoulder.

I surveyed the team we were heading out with. Ramon, with a pistol at his side, Dove, with a large stick in hand for fending off attacks, and Leroy, whose larger pack bulged with the necessary items Ramon had insisted upon. The rest of us carried only what was needed. Ammunition, a small hand-held radio to contact base in the case of a catastrophe, and food. We'd be seeking shelter along the way.

The gate opened wide, and we stepped out onto the asphalt as dawn came upon the neighborhood. Across the way lay the remains of the old shopping center. Liam and his men had reinforced it and now used the buildings to store food, clothing, and other essentials.

The nip in the air reminded me winter would soon be upon us, and I shivered. A second winter and the ravages of the apocalypse were more noticeable with the passage of time. It was obvious in the refuse strewn on the roads from offices that sat empty, abandoned buildings, and the wrecks of vehicles.

We plodded onward, Dove taking the lead while the guards in our group kept a watchful eye. We'd decided for the first day to keep as far from the main roads as possible, agreeing that we didn't want to arouse interest from those zombies wandering around aimlessly.

"You know, if it weren't for the zombies, we'd have a fair idea what the first settlers went through," commented Mick, a thirty-something man of indeterminate heritage.

Dove laughed. "You have a strange sense of history. There weren't roads and houses."

Mick colored up. "No, I mean we could be on our own, the first explorers into an area that's unknown and largely uninhabited by European settlement."

I cocked my head. "Good analogy. Mick, what did you do before all this?"

He sighed. "I was a butcher. Had a shop in Wanniassa. Did a roaring trade online until this all went down."

I wouldn't have pegged him as that. Maybe a philosopher or teacher given what he'd just said. I let the thought float away and concentrated on where I stepped and what lay around me.

We trudged on for what seemed like hours through the knee-high grass, threading between overgrown shrubs until we heard the noise we really wanted to avoid. The low moan of a calling zombie. It was met with the twin sound of a second, and I rubbed my brow.

As a group, we stilled and waited to see where it came from.

The dubious safety of a tree beckoned us, and we sheltered beneath the skeleton branches as Dove, Leroy, and I peered beyond our hiding place.

"Can you see anything?" I whispered, and Leroy shook his head.

"No. I need the binoculars."

I pulled the small pair from the pocket on the side of my pack and handed them to him.

Waiting silently, more than a little tense, until he exhaled was difficult. The sounds didn't bode well.

"Two. In a bad way, though, so should be easy to pick off. We clear them, then let Ramon take a look at what we find."

I hated this part, but I waited until Dove stepped back, then raised my rifle. A glance to my left told me Leroy had done the same. "I'll take the right," I muttered and found my mark, centered her in the eyepiece, and gently squeezed the trigger as I exhaled. The boom was joined by a second loud noise echo, and I watched as the zombie fell to the ground.

I lowered the firearm, nausea welling up. I controlled it. Barely.

"We should move," said Leroy as I noted the way his gaze settled on me.

"Yes. I need to take a look." Ramon strode forward, and we trailed along behind him. I watched from a distance as he knelt on the ground, slid on a set of disposable gloves, then poked and prodded at the corpses. He opened the eyes, and as always, the pale milky-ness of the orbs left me shuddering. When he opened the mouth, the stench was alarming, and we all moved back swiftly. Or at least, all but Ramon.

"Hmm. Looks like malnutrition, and it makes them no good for our purposes," he said. I frowned. "Malnutrition? How can that be?"

Ramon stood, stripped off the latex covering his hands, and surveyed the surroundings.

We stepped away and allowed Dove to do his thing as we discussed Ramon's musings. "There's not many bodies here. She possibly starved from lack of flesh as did her male counterpart. While they're technically dead, the body reanimates almost fully and is capable of both weight loss and gain, as we've ascertained over the last year. There is just a lack of high- level thought processes, verbal communication, and so on. Their actions tend to be limited to life sustaining."

I wasn't even game to ask how they'd come by that information. "What else are they capable of?"

He smiled. "Not reproduction at least."

One of the other guards gave a muffled kind of laugh, as if they were both horrified and fascinated by the answer.

I was thankful for the no-reproduction thing, but the concept left my brain whirring madly. "We should get moving, in case the shots alerted any more of these creatures that we're around."

On that we all agreed, and for the next little while we moved faster than we had all day.

Leroy

We camped the first night in an abandoned house. J found clean sheets and blankets, and locked and barred the doors and windows, then set about checking what in the house was worth salvaging. Clothing was packed into suitcases we found, toys discovered in one bedroom we shoved into rubbish bags, and canned goods plus dried foods were emptied into baskets we'd discovered in the laundry.

"We should mark the location on a map, so we know to come back here," Dove said, and I agreed with his comment.

"We'll grab the keys hanging on the rack. There may even be a car in the garage. We can check that in the morning and load it up if there is. Depending on if it's got petrol, we could drive it back to the compound."

For now, we all settled on the lounge floor, the small portable stove set up, and a couple of the men cooked the stew mix they'd brought with them.

Together, the group dragged bedding and cushions in the lounge, and we created makeshift pallets on the floor. "I never did slumber parties as a kid," said Julia, and the others simply shrugged. I wondered what else she hadn't done or experienced, but I remained silent.

"You know, when I first went on the road, I would have killed for this setup. But now that I'm used to a proper bed again, this is going to be hell on my back," I muttered.

Dove snickered and slid down on the cushions he'd found. He

closed his eyes, even though his lips moved as if deep in prayer. I wondered what he could possibly find to thank God for, but I kept my own counsel on that.

In the corner, on the mound of cushions we'd set up as a sentry post was Julia. I wondered if she'd welcome my company, but then, given we were surrounded by others in the party, I felt it wise to keep a distance.

When she glanced my way, I did smile slightly, then noted how her eyes widened, the shy corner turn-up that was almost a smile, and it settled the nerves that had taken up residence in my gut.

I burrowed down, well aware I'd be standing duty in the midnight hours and rest was imperative. I willed my breathing to slow and drifted off to be woken some time later by shoving at my arm.

"Wake up," whispered Julia in rattled tones.

"Wha—"

"Shh... I think there's something outside."

That blew the rest of the fog from my thoughts, and I climbed out of the makeshift bed, reaching for my pistol and shotgun and crawling across the room to the window.

I half-stood, peered through the grimy windows, and watched the play of artificial light bobbing outside. "Shit! Wake the others, but make sure they're silent."

As she did, I remained by the window, my gaze locked on the tableau. Ten or eleven people in armed service uniforms moved in the darkness, the lights bobbing up and down. I could feel the weight of the gazes of our team on my back, and I turned toward them, placed my hand over my mouth, indicating for silence, and then mimed for them to stay down.

The lights flickered in our direction, and we moved out of sight, me ensuring the curtains didn't move. We didn't want to be detected.

"Nothing there," I heard someone call, and the breath I'd held onto whooshed out.

The sound of feet pounding through dirt echoed as they

retreated, while I kept my watch. "Who the fuck was that?" demanded Julia.

"I'd guess they were military, given the uniforms and the way they moved. I'd like to get the specimens and get out of here," I added, wishing I knew more about what was going on.

With all of us roused, we gathered again around the small stove as Dove heated water for coffee. Those still needing the addition of milk added a little of the powdered item to their drinks.

No one spoke, which meant it was pretty eerie, then we took up a vigil until the first spearing fingers of dawn painted the sky.

Julia motioned me over. "We should go see if we can determine where they went."

I nodded, aware she needed a few minutes of privacy.

Once we'd donned our coats and packs, she slid around the door into the bracing air.

"Okay, so you clearly think they're military, Leroy. Or is there more?"

A sigh slipped out. "The guy in charge? He was in my group for the inoculation drop. Name of Hastings, Corporal Samuel. Straight as an arrow when it came to crawling up someone's ass. Some called him a brown noser, but I just called him dipshit. He was in everything for the glory. Not unintelligent, just uncreative."

When Julia frowned, I wondered what was going through her mind. "So, when you say *group*, you mean what exactly?"

"We were all sent to main cities. Those with reticulated water systems, because the smaller locations were too difficult to inoculate. We were initially told that those smaller places would be dealt with in the second wave. He was the first to take the vial. Said he'd been chosen because they already knew of him and his work ethic. At the time I had no clue, until it all made sense, then it was too late."

Her blank look made me pause.

"Clearly he was involved from the beginning. How he got chosen I can only speculate on." I scratched my head, looking out over the abandoned houses nearby. "He used to talk about his family connections..." And fool that I'd been, I hadn't considered he might actually be talking anything other than smack.

"You think he might be involved at a higher level?"

I turned back and shrugged. "I don't know. He said his brother worked in some politician's office, but I never paid too much attention." Inhaling deeply, I knew it was time to spill the thing that most worried me about what we'd seen. "The thing that worries me about this is they were on the hunt for someone or something. Given the little we've already learned, what's to say it wasn't us?"

"Oh God." Her voice sounded strangled, and she blanched. "You think they might be—"

"Yeah. We have to assume they're still on the case. We know the vaccine didn't work. We know my team was involved in the distribution that caused the virus. We know it certainly wasn't what I was informed it would be. The only thing we don't know is who ordered the virus."

"Then we need to stay off the radar. We get the others up and out. We stay away from any areas that could potentially house hostiles, then we get out of here, pronto."

We hurried back to the house, shared the news, and answered the queries we could give answers to.

"Why don't we just take the car then?" questioned Ramon, and I shook my head.

"Sound carries. If they are hostile in intention, we've just painted a bright red target on our forehead. We go forward on foot. Stick to the outskirts and stay alert."

It wasn't a great plan, but right now it was all we had.

Chapter 11

Julia

WE KEPT UP A RAPID PACE, searching for somewhere to hole up for the night, just as we had for the last five days. They'd been grueling and cold marches as we made our way closer to where we had heard the new zombies had congregated. My fingers were numb as we left the bushy scrub to enter the township we'd earmarked as tonight's camp.

The sound of a motor and vibrations of something moving swiftly had us drawing back into the bushes and out of sight.

I pulled out the binoculars and peered into the gloom. "Geez. This is not good," I moaned and handed the glasses to Leroy.

"Looks like military, but why would they be here?"

I wanted to ask that myself. Were they tracking us? After something or... Lightbulb moment. "*The zombies*. The ones who've evolved. What if they know we're looking for them?"

Leroy rocked back on his heels. "Why would they be doing that though? I mean, given the military was the instrument of the initial contagion, wouldn't they know?"

I bit my lip and turned to Ramon. "Why? Why would they be

rounding them up?" Indeed, the open-bodied cattle truck was full of moaning zombies. I turned back and watched the idling truck, my mind whirring with possibilities.

He harrumphed. "Maybe the mutation wasn't expected? There are so many variables, and if it was pushed out before all the tests were completed, they may have thought it ready for release because they took a shortcut on the trials. It depends if they were planning to release a secondary strain, one being the vaccine and the other strain it was meant to eradicate."

"You mean let some get infected and the vaccine being magically shared with the government riding in on a white stallion to save the day?" That was beyond sick and twisted, if that were indeed the case.

Leroy groaned. "Jesus, we were played like bloody violins."

Both Ramon and I turned to him. "What do you mean?"

"Each team was either an A or a B. I was an A Team member and we went out first, told to administer the liquid on the twenty-eighth of April. The B Teams were to move in on the third, as their vaccine payload was running behind. Or at least that's what they said."

"But only you dispensed in your given area, right?"

He sighed. "No. Team B was to re-inoculate later at those locations. We were told two teams would ensure full coverage and would result in a successful mission." Fury and self- loathing laced his words.

"Two inoculations?" Ramon inclined his head as if thinking through what was being suggested.

"You can't know what you were dispensing then, Leroy." I wanted to reassure him, sliding my hand down his arm in what I hoped was a soothing gesture. Beneath my touch, his arm was like pure steel, hard and unyielding.

There wasn't much to say at this point, and all we were doing was guessing and drawing our own conclusions. We could be totally off base with our summations, and I really hoped that was the case. Anything else meant someone had been willing to play the genocide card. But who?

"Julia is correct. You could have been dispensing the vaccine, but because the time period was too short if they released a second inoculation into the system only a few days after the initial dosing, it's no surprise the efficacy of the vaccine was undermined. If you were indeed dispensing the virus, I imagine you would have been required to wear hazardous material wear, and—"

Leroy snorted. "This is the army, Ramon. We were told to arrive in civvies. To wear normal street clothes, and if anyone asked, we were taking water samples for the government and to collect one if watched. It wasn't a regular mission where the normal guidelines applied."

Ramon rubbed his hands over his eyes. "Dammit, whoever was running this operation—"

"Should be flogged. I agree, Ramon. But right now, let's focus on what's going on down that road, shall we? We need one of those zombies." A second truck roared into view, and I watched, wondering what the hell they were up to as it pulled up and stopped. "Or at least a sample. What would work, Ramon? What do you need?"

"Tissue. A hand or similar, but we'd need to be quick."

I bit my lip. Here would be closer to home and faster to get it back. But the chances of being caught were more than a little concerning. "Leroy?"

His brow knit as if already understanding what I needed an answer to. "They aren't leaving the vehicles unattended. I'd suggest waiting."

Even as he spoke, men poured into the first vehicle, hanging off the doors, and the man with the clipboard climbed into the cab, then it drove off with a puff of smoke.

The driver of the second vehicle and the two men within climbed down and entered the building.

"Leroy?" I turned to him, but he was already standing, waving our other men over. Dove frowned. "What are you planning to do?"

"I'm going to get that sample," Leroy replied. "Stay here with Ramon and Julia. You others with me."

Leroy

I knew Julia would be worried. Hell, this was pretty damned risky given what we'd seen, but it was the best opportunity, and all we had to do was get a tissue sample.

So we brushed aside the undergrowth and slipped and slid our way down the bank. At the edge of the road, in front of the truck, we stilled and crouched down while I tugged a big ass knife from my pack. "Give me that bag," I muttered to the oldest man and sized up the contents of the van. They growled and moaned.

One caught sight of us and bared grayish-green teeth. The stench was putrid. There were men and women in that truck—or the remains of them—and a few pre-teen bodies. Milky white eyes stared as they gripped the metal and wood bars.

"Better be quick," someone muttered behind me.

"Just keep an eye out."

A hand reached out, gnarled and bony. I looked but decided against using that specimen.

Younger had to be better, right? I lurched into a standing position.

One of the zombies lunged. A male in prime condition. Clearly newly turned and strong.

He'd make an awesome candidate, I thought, and without time to second-guess or change my mind, I swung the machete. The jar was hard, and the thud loud enough to be audible to those of us gathered around the truck.

A screech filled the air, and other hands reached out, long nails barely missing my cheek as I moved back. The bag was used to scoop up that flesh, and even as we were closing a second bag around our specimen we were fleeing back to the hidden safety of the underbrush. We dove out of sight just as the door to the house opened. Hidden among the scratchy undergrowth, I watched, determined to ensure this mission was a success.

"What the fuck is going on?" the middle-aged driver screamed from the safety of the doorway, his glass of amber liquid sloshing over his fingers. "Shut up!"

I held my breath, hoping he wouldn't patrol the vehicle, not with the spray of black blood glistening on the side of the truck and the road. Meanwhile, inside the body of the truck, the zombie was going wild, his one hand clawed, eyes wide and staring at me.

"Good thing he's contained," said the man who now held the plastic bag with the body part, "otherwise I'd say you're dinner."

I nodded, but my stomach cramped at the reality of what I'd just done. "Better stash that straight away in the cooler box once we reach the others," I instructed, watching until the driver retreated inside. "Let's get out of here."

We hurried back to the rest of the team.

"Leroy?" Julia's eyes widened as she took in the wetness splashed over my shirt.

"Not mine."

Her eyes closed briefly, and I noted the moisture shaking on the tips of her eyelashes. "Okay, we should go."

I stopped her as the others huddled nearby. "You okay?"

She nodded without a word, but my hand on her shoulder reinforced how worried she'd been, the way her muscles under my touch jumped and twitched.

I took her hand in mine. "Come on."

We gathered up the team. "We need to be watchful. I have no idea if they have scouts, and night is settling in."

We moved together in the dusk, following our path back to last night's place of shelter, thankful the moon had risen high in the sky, giving us enough light that we didn't need to use torches. The chill factor became our largest concern, as we wrapped scarves around our lower faces and stuffed our hands deeply into pockets. Every now and again a sound would stop us in our tracks. On three occasions we dropped to the ground as lights or movement caught our attention.

The door creaked as we entered the building, an old service station, and I quietly gestured to some to check the building for others, or worse, zombies. On their return, I barricaded the doors, and we retreated to the middle room.

Ramon took the cooler box now and investigated what I'd done. "Clean enough."

Julia looked away, and not for the first time I wondered how the hell she had the fortitude to cope with her role in this wild new world.

"I'll take first watch," I said. And everyone except Julia nodded.

They made up their pallets on the floor and settled in. We wouldn't have long to sleep; the need to move at dawn drove me on.

"Are you okay?" I asked her once the sounds of even breathing and snores filled the air.

"Yeah. I just... I was worried. You were gone, and I couldn't see very well. When the second truck came, I was afraid you'd be caught up in whatever is going on." Her voice broke just a little.

I slid my arm around her, and for a moment she stiffened, then released the pressure between us with a sigh.

"I don't want to lose you, Leroy. I mean, I don't exactly know what we have, but it means something to me."

The lump in my throat came pretty close to strangling me. "I... Yeah. Me too. But I wasn't sure until now, and I'm here for the long haul." Realization burst inside me. I wasn't planning on going anywhere. The sensation of being home had crept up and caught me unawares.

Julia

The second day back was long and difficult. The weather turned bitter, and the wind nearly cut us in half.

"We're going to have to find shelter," I told Leroy, but a harsh look settled on his face.

"We need to keep moving. They'll work out what happened soon enough, and we need to get Ramon and the specimen squared away before they come looking for us."

Ramon was flagging by the middle of the day, but Leroy pushed us on. We only managed a ten-minute break for morning tea and lunch and passed our safe house in the middle of the afternoon.

By dusk I'd had enough. "Stop, Leroy!" He turned.

"We can't keep this pace up. Ramon isn't like us, and the team is dragging out too far." I pointed to the stragglers, their weary steps leaving them well behind the leaders. "If we're attacked, we aren't close enough together to be able to help. This isn't like you, Leroy. What's going on?"

He shook his head and sighed. "They'll come looking for us. We need to get as far away as we can."

That wasn't everything though. Not by a long shot. "Why? Why are you pushing us suddenly? You haven't taken into account the members of the team. You're worried. I get that, because I am too."

"I knew the guy in charge, or at least his type. The one with the clipboard? He's military. Won't give a damn about anything except finding us. Now, we've bought some time because the driver wasn't going anywhere. But even if we account for that, we only have maybe an extra twelve hours. Once they get to wherever the cargo will be checked. Inspected."

I knew then what his concern was. "They've got vehicles."

"Yeah. They'll come looking. Once they see the clean cut of the zombie, they'll know someone is aware of whatever it is they're doing."

"This way won't work though, Leroy."

"We need to get closer. Once we find the shelter I should be within range to hail Liam. Get Ramon and the specimen home."

When his gaze settled on me I saw the fear in his eyes. He felt responsible for me, and that emotion filled some cavern inside me. The one I didn't even know was empty. It felt a whole heap like...*love*. It was as if the universe decided to drop a great big bomb on me at a time when I was unable to do anything about it. We had men, responsibilities, and a bloody hand stuffed in a cooler to deliver in the hopes of creating a vaccine.

"Oh fuck!" I whispered, and he reached out, took my hand.

"What?"

I shook my head. "Not now, Leroy. But when we get home, we need to talk."

He gave me a look that said 'I have no idea what you're talking about, but that sounds serious'.

I shrugged it off because now wasn't the time or the place. Instead, I simply hitched up my backpack. "We should keep moving then." So we did.

Darkness came, the temperatures settling lower than before, and the few times we spoke steam filled the air. We banded together now, arms twined around each other so we could assist those in danger of falling over. More than once we stumbled, and some fell to the ground with an *oomph*. I kneaded my legs which ached and noted others doing the same. What I wouldn't give for some liniment right now, I thought with a snort.

Ramon was my biggest concern though. He huffed and puffed, and he'd become unsteady on his feet. "Not long now, Ramon," I told him, and he smiled weakly.

"Not sure how you do this regularly," he answered as I held his hand.

"Last push and we'll be there." *God, I hope so!* I wasn't sure how much further we could push him, but move we did, although at a much slower pace now.

Sometime around midnight we saw the first of the safe houses we'd bunked down in for this mission. We shoved inside without checking as energy had run low. We barred the doors and pulled the curtains tight.

The ground shook, and a sound, a roar, grew. "Upstairs," Leroy urged us, and we dragged our packs up. Lights shone bright, and we moved into the relative shelter of the hall, all torch light extinguished.

Leroy dropped to the floor, and I followed suit, crawling across the old carpet as dust rose in my nostrils. I had to work at not sneezing as I made it to the nearest window then slid against the wall as we rose.

"Stay out of sight," he warned me as I peered through the grimy glass.

A truck passed by slowly. A body truck, like that which had carried the zombies.

"Is it them?" I asked, fearful at Leroy's expected answer.

"Yeah."

My fingers curled over the butt of my pistol still safe in its holster at my waist.

Time passed slowly until the vehicle moved on and my breathing became almost normal again. *Almost* because every sound now had me sucking air into my aching lungs, expecting the worst.

"We should bed down up here tonight. No lights, just keep these curtains open for light. Double the guard."

Leroy's suggestion sounded good, so I nodded. "One on the stairs and one here."

We arranged our watches, and I tugged an old mattress from the bed. Dust flew up in plumes, and we coughed until the air cleared somewhat. Once I'd settled my bedding on it, I scanned the walls of the room. It was a boy's den; motorbike images and the occasional scantily clad female graced the walls as did models of planes and bikes.

"Leroy?"

"Hmm?"

"You found a car, right?"

"A people mover. In the garage."

"What about motorbikes?" I rolled over to look at his face. He'd screwed it up, thinking.

"No, but there were helmets."

"Was there a shed outside?"

"Out back, sure. We didn't look too closely at it though. Why?"

I smiled. "It appears whoever lived here was a motorbike fanatic. Helmets. So where's the bike or bikes? Clearly, if there are helmets, someone is riding, right? And you said helmets as in more than one. Stands to reason there could be more than one bike in storage."

"God, you're good." He pulled me close into a hug. As the explosion of hunger roared through my system, I wanted more. Now wasn't the time or the place though.

"Let's not get our hopes up just yet. But maybe we'll be able to carry everyone comfortably."

We settled in, and the night passed uneventfully.

Leroy

I'd considered Julia's words for a long time, and by the time we'd risen, packed our bags, and hurried downstairs the need to check the contents of the shed became an all-consuming hunger, because if it did indeed contain motorbikes, I knew that meant a better chance of success.

Carefully, I cracked open the back door; Ramon, Dove, and Julia just behind me. We scanned the exterior, though all was still quiet, and hotfooted it to the shed. Locked.

"Did anyone see anything we can use to open this with?"

"No, but we could shoot the lock off. I mean, that would work, right?" Ramon grinned, and I looked at him.

"Seriously? Like that happens in movies, and I never took you for a thrill seeker."

Ramon shrugged. "I've grown to like action movies since the plague."

"No. For two reasons. One, someone could get hurt, and two, it might bring interest down on us that we aren't prepared for."

The laughter in Ramon's eyes melted away at my harsh words, but the truth was, I didn't want to stay any longer than we absolutely had to. We were sitting ducks.

"Let me check the garage. There could be some bolt cutters on the tool rack."

Julia scurried away, and Dove followed her, as did my gaze. "You like her."

I started at Ramon's careful words. "Maybe, but right now, she's in charge and we have to get out of here."

"True. But in these times, you have to act fast, because there may not be a tomorrow. I learned that early on. Take the chance, Leroy."

He was right, but I had so little to offer her at this point. I'd been part of the plot that caused this plague. Not in a position to make decisions, but I'd been one of those who'd carried out the mission. How could I in all honesty now offer her my heart when it was tainted?

I rubbed my hand over my aching eyes, and here came Julia and Dove, carrying a large bolt cutter. "It was in the garage. We should pack the rest of the tools too. Take them back with us in case we need them."

Taking the cutters, I applied them to the lock. It crunched down, broke the lock, and I pulled it off. Then I opened the doors.

No bikes. "Dammit, there should have been something here. Something useful."

Julia stepped inside. "Nothing much we can use by the looks of it." Her shoulders slumped, and I knew she'd been so hopeful.

I spied two small cans in the corner, lifted them, and smiled. "Gas!"

"Great," Dove said, and he scooped them out of my hands. "I'll take it to the garage. The men are grabbing what we can carry and loading up now."

"I'll go with him," added Ramon, and he retreated, leaving Julia and I alone in the yard together.

"I was so sure." She closed the shed with a sigh. "Why can't something be easy for a moment?"

I rubbed her shoulder in what I hoped was a reassuring manner. "We'll get back to the compound and go forward from there."

"Yeah."

The sunlight, weak and watery, settled on something behind the shed. A glint of metal caught my eye.

"Don't be so down yet, Julia. There's something back here."

I shouldered past the overgrown bushes, and they scratched, drawing blood. More than just determined, I pushed on. Behind the shed was a canvas covered trailer. It was the A-Frame I'd caught sight of, followed by the faded green canvas that covered the boxy tray.

"What's this?" I grabbed the corner of the tarpaulin and hauled it back. In the cage sat three dirt bikes.

Maybe I should be thanking God and talking to Dove, I thought, feeling a loosening of the weight that had borne down on me.

"Ever ridden a motorbike?" I asked.

Julia grinned. "Maybe. Maybe not."

I laughed and ran a finger down her cheek, giving in to the need to touch her. "If you have, that's great, you and I can ride one if they go. And if not, here's your chance to learn. We can use the trailer to cart what we've found behind the people mover, and the bikes will get three of us back comfortably. Let's get some help and get them out of here."

As we hurried into the house, I grabbed her hand. "What are you doing, Leroy?"

"Nothing." But Ramon's words chased around in my head. *Act quick. Don't waste a chance.*

At the door I called for Dove. "What do you know about using tree cutters things?"

"Tree cutters?" Dove shook his head. "I need more information."

"We've got a trailer and three dirt bikes. We'll need to cut the greenery so we can pull it out. Hook it onto the people mover," Julia explained.

"There were tree loppers in the garage. I'll grab them."

Dove left us at a run, and I took the opportunity to pull Julia close and loop my hands over her shoulders. "Get the men to load the trailer as quickly as you can, then get the helmets. We'll need to check to make sure they start and have gas. Since they were stored in a caged trailer, hopefully the keys will be in the ignition. We're going to have to move quickly though."

"Yeah, okay. I'll get Ramon to pack the tissue sample in the front of the van. You and I on bikes. If we don't have a third..."

"Ask Dove. He's a man of many talents."

Julia's eyes widened. "Look, about Dove——"

The urge overwhelmed me, and I found myself pulling her head to mine and kissing her. I tried to keep it light, but the hunger that never really went away scorched me. "Not now," I whispered against her mouth. "Later. Back at the compound."

Her hands covered mine. "You bet. We've got some stuff to discuss. But I need you to know, I have no intention of ignoring this thing between us."

She grinned and moved away before heading for the back door.

Julia

The bikes worked, although it initially took some effort to get them to start. We'd loaded the trailer and hooked it to the car, and thankfully, it started with the first try. Everyone loaded up, and I pulled on the helmet Leroy passed to me. It was tighter than I would have liked, but I refused to ride bare-headed so I shrugged it off. At least mine was pink. Hot pink with silver unicorn decals.

We'd agreed that Dove, Leroy, and I would ride ahead of the van, and we'd radio in closer to the compound. That way we could react faster if we came across the truck. I just hoped we didn't.

"Let's ride," I called, and Dove laughed as I throttled up.

My hands curled around the handles as we rode out of the yard. Truthfully, I hadn't been on a dirt bike, or any kind of motorbike, since I was sixteen and going out with Freddy McClure. I snorted with laughter remembering his pimple face and earnest blue eyes. I wondered what happened to him, then looked over to my right. Leroy rode beside me, already comfortable on his red and blue unit, and Dove on the orange one brought up the rear.

We'd plotted a course, fairly straight, which would take us back to the compound in under two hours. I just hoped we had enough gas in the tanks, but Leroy had checked and was sure we'd make it. Besides, we'd loaded the full cans into the vehicle behind us.

The day was cool and crisp, as if some great being understood the need to be fast. After two and a half days on the road, we needed to get that specimen into use before it degraded too much. We needed Ramon back behind the safety of the compound fence, and I needed to clear the air with Leroy.

All in a day's work, really.

Chapter 12

Leroy

THE RIDE WAS STRANGELY quick and painless. I radioed in about twenty minutes out, and we'd seen no signs of a military unit.

We roared into the compound, the doors slid shut behind us, and I pulled in the first full breath I'd managed since leaving that house.

Liam came out to meet us. "Well, you've brought bounty with you, I see. What about the specimen?"

I watched as Julia clambered off her bike and rounded the vehicle to accept the precious cargo from Ramon. "Right here," Ramon said.

"Good work, team. Ramon, bring it in. I've got a team arriving tomorrow, but if you've got something to do..." Liam waved his hands, and I waited as Julia sauntered over to me. "Well, the rest of you deserve a day off. Go get some food, a shower, and a change of clothing. We can meet for a debrief after—"

"Not quite that simple, Liam. We've got a rather large problem, and you need to know about it sooner rather than later," my girl told him.

Liam blinked. "All right then. Come inside and I'll organize some coffee."

The two of us followed him inside after assuring the others they could go take some downtime. It felt odd to be coming in from the field to what was essentially a very homey kitchen and office setup. I knew we stank, and I particularly was covered with dried blood, but we needed to tell him straight away about the military movements.

Elaine left the three of us settled at the table even though I'd said I really shouldn't sit down.

"Liam, there's military or pseudo military out there. They're gathering up the zombies. We don't know where they're taking them, just that they've got them all in trucks, like cattle, and they're shipping them elsewhere." Julia spoke quickly, and I nodded, the whole time watching Liam for his reaction.

Liam's face turned stony. "How far away?"

I dug out my map. "We were here when we saw them." I pointed to the location, and he rubbed a tic above his left eye. "They'd gathered them up, which is why I was able to get the sample we have. The guy in control of the second truck had gone inside." I explained the rest of the situation, the truck we'd seen last night. "Have you seen any trucks in the vicinity?"

Liam shook his head. "We're too big for most militia to bother with, it would seem. But we need to know more."

"Liam? We were talking, and Leroy and I think that they're rounding up those that have evolved. Perhaps to test them or to experiment on them. Which is bad enough, but what if they're behind the evolution? What if it's a continuation of the initial plan?"

Her hand gripped mine really tight as Liam glanced at me, aghast. "Do you think that's likely?"

"The only thing I know for certain is the guy in the first truck is military. I saw the way he moved. If he's not from the unit I was co-opted to, I'd be very surprised. If that's the case, he'll want and need that tissue sample. They'll find us soon enough, and when they do—"

"We'll be ready, Leroy. Now go. Downtime for you both."

Chapter 13

Julia

WE WALKED BACK SLOWLY. Not touching, but there wasn't a lot of space between us. No one spoke to us. We didn't gain anyone's interest, and that suited me just fine, because the roiling in my gut and the nerves that settled in my chest would have made speech impossible.

At the steps of the building, I stopped, turned, and looked at Leroy. "Will you come up with me?" I knew exactly what I was offering and breathed a little easier when his gaze roamed my face then he gave a nod. He knew too.

I fumbled in my pocket for the key, which he removed from my nerveless fingers and unlocked the unit.

We stumbled inside. The interior was cool, and I shivered.

"Are you all right?" he asked, and I nodded.

"Shut the door." My words wobbled a little, but he pushed the wood closed so we were alone in the silence.

I stripped off my dirty jacket and dropped it on the floor. There'd be time to deal with that after.

"Julia," he whispered.

I lay my finger against his lips, stilling his words. I didn't want to talk, not yet. I just needed to feel him. His strength surrounding me was the one thing I'd craved during the mission. We'd both denied ourselves that though, because we knew how it would end.

Leroy's arms wound around me, and I simply rested my head against his chest, listening to the steady thud of his heart.

"What are we doing here, Julia?" The timbre of his words echoed in his chest and set off tiny fireworks of sensual hunger inside me.

I tugged away and looked at him. "You know I want you, Damien Leroy."

"Yes."

He remained immovable, like a boulder, and I sighed. "I want more than that though. More than just a quick session of sex. I heard what Liam said about procreating and children, and that... I want that someday, but not yet. I want time with you. To be with you and to learn about you and us."

He frowned, and I wondered what he was thinking in that moment. "All right." But his gaze remained clouded as if he were unsure where I was going with this.

God, I'm making a mess of this! "Leroy, I feel deeply for you. I mean, when you disappeared down there to get the specimen I felt like—"

"I understand," he whispered.

I shook my head, tears burning beneath my now tightly closed lashes. "No. I knew then that if anything happened to you, I'd just wither away. That I couldn't lose you. That I..." The words stuck in my throat. "I...I love you, Damien Leroy!"

The silence grew. The quiet was unbearable, because I'd just bared my soul to him and he didn't say anything. Mortification burned me, my face flaming hot, and I ducked down, wishing myself a million miles away.

When his hand took mine, I tried to snatch it away, but then I caught sight of him, the tears rolling down his cheeks, and I stopped.

He was crying. Silently shaking as if an integral part of his being had been smashed.

"Leroy? Are you all right?" Terror replaced the fear, and I reached up, cupped his cheek with my shaking hand. "Talk to me, because you're scaring me."

He laughed, shaky and uncertain. "I'm lost for words. I love you too. It surprised me when I realized it, but you didn't seem to be interested in anything long-term, and I... I've made decisions and done things..." He tried to pull away, but I stopped him. "Things that no one could possibly love me for."

The need to reassure overcame rational thought. "We all have. Since the outbreak, the laws and morality have changed. We've changed. Nothing is the same. We did what we had to in order to survive."

"It doesn't undo what I did before," he bellowed as he stepped away. The distance chilled me as much as the self-loathing in his voice. "I don't deserve you, or this." He waved his hands at the small apartment. "Any of it."

"Why? Because you followed orders?"

Fury sizzled in my veins. He'd followed the bloody orders he'd been given. Now he had to live with the knowledge of the consequences because some fucking arse in Canberra wanted to be prime minister and run the whole fucking show. It wasn't good enough that they could be scared, because in that moment I wanted them to *pay*. But Damien Leroy was suffering now, before me, and he was my priority.

"You didn't know what they were doing, you merely carried out the task you were told to do. You weren't the only one to follow orders, but you're the one helping us find a way forward now, when it counts. Nothing can change what's already happened, but we can learn and be better people because of our experiences." God, I hoped he was listening, because it was breaking me into tiny bits to listen to him tear himself apart with guilt.

"I don't..." He slid to the floor, hands over his face, shoulders convulsing in front of my gaze. "Then I had to take that hand, and I just..." Leroy quieted now and sighed.

I knelt down. "I know. I understand what you're saying, if not exactly how you feel, but you don't have to do it anymore. No more missions for either of us, Leroy. I'll talk to Liam, but you need help, and I'm here. For you. Always for you."

"Fuck. You must think I'm some kind of weakling," he groaned, swiping at his face.

"No. I think you're a good man who's trying to deal with a situation you didn't invite or want. You need help to come to terms with this, and tomorrow we'll go see Ramon, together. But for now, know that I'm here and not going anywhere."

He rose, his face averted.

I tugged him toward my tiny bathroom. "Come on and have a warm shower, then I'll organize some food for us both."

"Julia..." He gripped the doorway, ceasing my push as he turned. "Thank you. I've never lost it like that. Not ever."

Unable to stop myself, I rose on tiptoes and kissed him gently. "I guessed as much. But you don't have to tough it out on your own anymore. That's what people in love do for each other."

Leroy

I ate slowly, picking at the pasta dish Julia had organized. It wasn't that I wasn't hungry, but embarrassment chewed at me. Julia sat opposite me, watching me as I shifted food around my plate.

"If you've had enough, I can pop your plate in the fridge," she offered.

"Yeah, sure."

Before I could shove away from the table she was out of her seat and leaning over me. "Damien?"

"Yeah?"

"Would you maybe talk to Dove? He's a priest and might be able to, you know, ease your mind a little."

Ouch! Talk about difficult decisions. Dove was three-quarters in love with the woman I intended to sleep beside tonight and forever, if she'd have me. On the flip side, baring my soul to him might ease the pain of knowledge. Or would it? The indecision was almost worse than the truth of what I'd done.

"Maybe," I temporized, and she laughed; the first true laugh I'd heard from her since we'd returned home.

"He's not going to tell on you, Leroy. He's a priest, with the sanctity of confession and all that."

"Maybe." But I refused to be drawn further. If that path was the one I decided on...well, that would come in its own time.

Instead I took her plate, carried it to the sink, then turned and tugged her into my arms.

"Right now, I'd rather not talk." I leaned in to kiss her, letting it deepen so that our mouths ground together, and my hands slid around her figure to cup her butt.

Her legs wound around me, clasping me in an intimate embrace, and the heat that constantly licked at me burst into flame. Hunger surged in my veins, urging me to more and greater intimacy.

I moved to the benchtop and balanced her there, dragging my lips from hers. With shaking fingers, I reached for the buttons of her shirt, and she watched, eyes glazed and lips swollen from my efforts. *God! She's so hot!* I was so ready for her, I was almost ready to explode, my cock pushing against my briefs.

"Undo my belt and jeans, Julia," I croaked against her neck as my hands tugged at the round, plastic buttons.

"Ohhh..." She moaned and twined in my arms. "I will..."

The feel of her hands traveling down my body fanned the electricity zinging in every nerve ending until I felt the tug and release of constricting denim and leather. I hissed with pleasure as she burrowed her fingers beneath the cotton of my briefs. Her fingers tangled with the hairs then slid lower.

I groaned and threw back my head. "We have to slow down."

"Why?" She giggled a little, and I closed my eyes at the throaty sound.

"Because I won't last." Instead of waiting for a response, I stepped back, pushed my pants down and my briefs. "Come with me," I echoed her earlier words, well aware that she knew what I was doing.

She slid from the counter top and followed me to the bedroom where I tugged at her clothes so that we were both bare. Once more we came together—skin against skin. My hands shook as I traced one beautiful breast, the ripe berry nipple distended for me. The need to taste her flesh was a ravening beast inside me. *Control. Control. Control.* That chanting reminder that we had all night wasn't working for me so well though.

Her knees shook; I felt that movement against my sensitized legs and closed my eyes on a moan. "I'm going to make love with you, Julia."

"Yes."

The kiss was magical, hot and urgent as I gripped her waist, lifted her, and she slid those luscious legs around me. My cock nudged her labia and slid deeply within her hot, wet sheath.

"*Fuck*," I groaned as pleasure cascaded over me.

"Please. Please. Please." Her gasping words filled the air, urging the now rapid movements as flesh slapped and the urgent grip of fingers became all-consuming.

My chest heaved as I fought to give her satisfaction, aware that my own was looming ever closer. "Come for me," I demanded, and she did.

Julia splintered in my arms. The cry of completion teamed with the wild sensation of intimate milking, and I came with a rush I'd never before known.

She slid out of my arms, and we tottered to the bed, collapsed.

"We didn't make it all the way," she murmured.

"Are you sure about that?" I was so tired I could barely open my eyes, but I heard her bark of laughter.

"I meant to the bed."

"We didn't need it, Julia." I squinted at her, brushed a curl from her face. "Marry me." The words slipped out, and even though my first thought was *too soon*, it was quickly chased away by the beatific smile that filled her countenance.

"Yes. But not yet. We still need time."

I nodded. She was right. But we still sealed the promise with a kiss.

Julia

The next morning, I woke with an unfamiliar, yet very welcome weight spread across me. His question from last night echoed in my mind. Marry him. God knew I wanted to, but my concerns now were solely for Leroy.

I watched the way the sunlight played over his features. They were so relaxed in sleep, and I realized now I'd never seen him so quiet. I slid one finger down his cheek, delighting in the rough texture of his early morning growth.

His lips captured my finger, and his eyes opened.

"Good morning," I whispered, and he smiled, releasing the digit.

"It is indeed. Any morning that features you beside me is perfect." The words turned my belly to mush.

"Just so long as you're beside me, that's all I'll ever ask." I meant every word and watched as he levered up next to me, reached behind his neck, and removed the chain that hung there.

"What are you doing?"

"Taking this off." He held up the chain and ring he'd given to another woman. "I wore it to remind me of someone else. Someone I lost long ago, but now know I didn't love. Not as she deserved, and not like I do you. You're my future, Julia." He laid the items on the bedside table and turned back to me, framing my face with his hands.

His kiss was soft and sweet, a promise, and tears stung my eyes. "I love you too, Damien Leroy. No other man means as much to me as you do. Or ever could."

"Okay then. Before we go any further, I also want to tell you how jealous I was of Dove. He's in love with you."

I slumped back on the pillows, my gaze searching the ceiling.

"He and I were thrown into a number of sticky situations, but it's not love like this, Leroy. I think it's more that he's afraid that he will always be alone, and he's a good man." I tugged the comforter close around my body, wondering how much I could say. "He returned to his school after the zombies attacked the hospital the first time. Got in and fought some off, but the girls of his school weren't so lucky. My team rescued him. He'd been hiding in the sacristy, and initially his relief had him latching onto the only female of the team. He thought that was love, but it was like a survivor's syndrome kind of thing. I can't really explain it properly. I kept him in my team because I understood his problem. He refused to fight, and some wanted to turn him out because he wasn't useful. It was horrible really. So, I kept him close, and safe, because it was all I could think of." Tears burned as I remembered. "He's my friend though."

"I understand that now." Leroy slid closer to me and gathered me into his arms. "When we're ready, maybe he'd marry us?"

I bit my lip, and Leroy groaned.

"Do that and I'm going to go crazy."

"What?" I batted my eyelids, and he released a long sigh of frustration.

"Bite your lip again in that sexy fashion."

Of course, that was a gauntlet I couldn't ignore, and he responded in kind. The loving was soft. Full of laughter and careful, sliding touches until he filled me, feeding the ignited hunger that grew inside me until the need expanded and enveloped me.

"Damien, I love you." Our gazes meshed as he moved against me, my body sensitized and wound tight. The scent of sex filling the air with musk and hunger urged me to undulate against him, to glory in the way he filled me completely.

When I splintered in his arms, he joined me, our exhalations entwined.

In the aftermath, I lay boneless beside him, the covers on the floor, and my heartrate slowing with the languor of fulfilment. It had been so right. Every touch and—

"Shit," I murmured as realization burned me.

"What's wrong?" Leroy pushed a curl from my face, his gaze worried.

"No protection."

He laughed then. It wasn't the response I expected.

"Well, if you're pregnant, I guess I could make an honest woman of you."

I punched him, gently, in the shoulder. "We can cross that bridge when we come to it. If we get there anytime soon."

Chapter 14

Leroy

IT TOOK every ounce of willpower to knock on Dove's door. Not because I didn't want to talk to the man. I did. I just wasn't sure exactly what this would become. Baring my soul didn't come easily, or at least to others who weren't Julia.

Military men didn't do that, was the old way of thinking, and no matter what anyone else said, that ethic continued to permeate those of us scarred by our service. Or at least, that's what my CO had said. But hell, I could no longer be sure if that was an accurate reflection or not, given my last mission.

Dove answered the door, his face crinkled. "What's up, Leroy?"

My tongue stuck in my mouth like a dried sponge on a pot. "I, uh... I want to talk to you. If I can?"

He opened the door wide. "Come on in then."

The closing of the door after me held a symbolic importance.

Dove indicated the seat just inside, an old armchair. "Would you like a cup of tea maybe?"

It seemed surreal. "I, uh, coffee would be great."

He strode over to the small kitchenette. "What do you want to talk about?"

"I'm struggling, and Julia suggested you might be the best person to talk to about what I've done."

For a moment, Dove kept his counsel, pouring boiling water into the mug. "Milk?"

I shook my head, and he carried the two cups over to the small coffee table and lowered himself to the seat.

"Well, you've told me bits and pieces, and I've gleaned some too," he said. "But how about you start at the beginning."

The words came slowly, every one a knife of such sharpness it cut me to the bone. "I was part of the group that was involved in the spread of the virus. I was told that we were specifically chosen, and the mission was of great importance but covert. No one should know. I didn't understand the ramifications until it was too late. They didn't tell us that millions would die because of our actions. Men, women, and children who'd done nothing more than go about their daily lives. I'm a murderer, and yet Julia sees something in me, something I don't. I'm not worthy of her, yet she—"

Dove held up his hand. "If you'd known the ramifications, would you have followed through?"

I squinted. "What do you mean?"

"If you'd had a choice, and could have said no. If you'd known everything you know now, would you have followed through?"

"No. No!" I rose, and the hot coffee I held in my hand spilled over me, burning. I dropped the cup on the floor, and it smashed. Just like so many lives I'd ruined.

"Don't worry about that for the moment," Dove said as if he read my mind. "I'm not a counselor. I don't profess to be one, and I'm not qualified for that. The only thing I can do is say to you that you're a good man. Like the cup on the floor, you were damaged by circumstances beyond any you could control."

I wanted to argue. To tell him he was wrong, and yet it made sense.

"I can't fix you. The only one in the end that can, is you. But you've shown you're not a mindless killer. You carry remorse for your actions. You grieve for what you've done. Daily you undertake tasks to make life better for those left behind. That makes you a flawed human, yes. Now it's time for you to believe that."

"I need to do more, Dove. It's not enough. But I..." I could barely string together a coherent sentence to explain just how much the actions of the past impacted me. "I can't go back out there and kill anymore. I can't..." The emotions I tried so hard to harness rose up again, drowning me.

"Then you must tell Liam. He too is a good man, and he'll understand."

***

Julia

We walked together as a group to the office cum house of Elaine and Liam. We hadn't chosen this consciously, we just all met near the old school building and walked as a team. This would be the last time, and as we neared the house I stopped as did they.

"I'm retiring from my role as a guardian," I announced. "Both Leroy and I have come to the conclusion that we can't do this anymore."

Leroy linked his fingers with mine and smiles broke out on faces.

"We kinda figured that out," one of them said.

"Oh." My face flamed. "I just didn't want you to hear it secondhand."

With nothing more to say, we resumed our journey. I knocked on Liam's door, and it opened wide to admit us.

"Good. Glad you're here for your debrief. Come in."

He led us into the converted lounge, and we took up positions on the couches.

I spoke candidly about what we'd seen. The zombies on the trucks, the men who were rounding them up. Sometime around here, the door opened, and the commandant and my stepfather, Allan, entered the room. The commandant pinned me with cold eyes, and I shivered in reaction. Leroy drew me close, and the scrutiny of Allan burned. I wasn't going to tell Liam in front of these men that we would no longer hunt. We'd now given our allegiance to this compound.

We finished the debrief and rose. As we began to file out, the commandant called both myself and Leroy to wait. We did, my stomach a congealing mass of nerves.

"So, you'll be returning to Queanbeyan now, J." Those words were an order, and I froze.

"No." My hand fisted. I was done with the orders that made me nothing more than a tool without a soul. Right here, I'd found my place. Giving back to this community, being part of it. I wasn't going anywhere.

His face turned hard, and he leaned forward, nostrils flaring. "I don't think you understand, Julia. Your posting—"

"She's now a valued member of my community, commandant. She and Leroy both have a home here." Liam spoke quietly, yet there was a firm resolve in his words.

My bones turned watery. Could it really be that simple?

Allan strode forward, and his eyes glinted. "Perhaps we might come up with a compromise? Julia continues to—"

Liam shook his head. "She's made her wishes clear. She has no further wish to hunt, isn't that right, Julia?"

I nodded enthusiastically, my hand still gripping Leroy's.

"You exceed your authority, Liam. These hunters are required back at our base." The commandant spoke firmly, but it was clear Liam wasn't going to budge.

"Look, I've given you time, but I refuse to allow my people to be pushed into something they cannot and should not be doing. Leroy has chosen to remain here along with the priest, Dove, and Julia." Liam's voice turned peevish. "So, unless there is something else, gentlemen?"

Allan gifted me with a soft smile. "Yes, my wife is here. If I could stay a couple of days?"

Liam inclined his head in agreement, and both men left the room, the commandant stomping and still furious he hadn't gotten his own way. *We'll need to tread carefully there, for a while.*

"So, since you're both staying, what will you do?"

I bit my lip. "I'd really like to finish the census task. Then I think I'd like to consider another more serious role."

Liam waited, but at this point I had no intention of telling him motherhood sounded good. I'd be employed in my task for many months yet, and I refused to rush anything.

"Besides," I said, "I think Leroy could do with—"

"Actually, I'm enjoying working with the children, but I would like to broaden the scope. Maybe start training others? We—I mean you—need more people trained as guards, and the women could do with some basics in self-defense."

Liam nodded. "True. Those plans sound fine. Now, with regards to housing, is there any need to change?"

I couldn't help but laugh and shot a look at Leroy who shared my mirth. "Maybe not yet. We'll let you know when."

"I'd also like to see Ramon. I've got..." Leroy cleared his throat as shades of scarlet rose fingerlike up his cheeks. "I think I need some help."

"All right. You know where his lab is."

Dismissed, we trailed outside, and I stopped, surprised to see Dove waiting nearby. "Dove? Is something wrong?"

"No, I'm just waiting to see Liam. I've been thinking about what we saw. I mean, with the evolved zombies. It occurs to me we know someone in government gave the directive for the disease to be released. We know their testing wasn't done properly, and the inoculations days later didn't work or didn't have time to take effect. But who was it at the head? Millions died, and someone has to be accountable, right? And the military or some are embroiled. Now we've got these evolving zombies. What if they're still part of the initial group who came up with this plan?"

"Oh God." I swiped an unsteady hand over my eyes. "Somehow, someone has to stop them."

"What if the commandant knows who it is?"

Now the fury inside me turned frigid, swiping those frozen tendrils up and down my back. "Oh God..."

Leroy shook his head. "I can't, Dove."

Dove smiled at us. "No. You need to heal, both of you, but I think you're on the right track. Together." Then Dove kissed me on the cheek. "Come see me when you're both ready."

Before I could laugh, he turned and headed to the door, hit it with three sharp raps, then entered. The door closed behind him, symbolic in my mind that we too had moved on.

If you enjoyed this book by Imogene Nix why not check out some more of her titles by scrolling through to the following pages?

Inheritance Of The Blood by
Imogene Nix

In the darkness evil waits…

As a young bride Kira was whisked away from everything and
everyone she knew, including her new husband and became
Christina, an operative of the Displaced Persons Unit.

As the danger grows she sees an opportunity to save her

husband Vasya and sister Serina. But nothing is the same. Serina is grown up—married and pregnant.

Vasya too is older and darkly forbidding. Trusting Christina doesn't come easily until a catastrophic event takes place. Now, knowing the truth everything he thought he knew is changed. But at a very high cost.

The four must work together to defeat the Demon, Zuor and the stakes are higher than they imagined and all could be lost.

The burning at the back of her neck warned she was being watched. A quick glance didn't clarify it. Instead, she turned around in time to see her mother's face, pale. "Mama?"

She took a step forward, but her grandfather snatched her wrist.

The grip was painful, and Kira stilled. "Let your parents talk."

She didn't know what the topic of conversation was, but it couldn't be good.

The dappled sunlight seemed cooler than before.

Her father crooked his forefinger at her grandfather while they stood there. For a moment she wished Vasya had come with them, but he had to work. Just the thought of her new husband warmed Kira.

She only had a few minutes to contemplate her newly defined status as a married woman, when her grandfather pulled at her hand. "Come with me." He tugged and, confused, Kira allowed herself to be towed away.

A glance at her parents' faces stole any feeling of well-being.

"Grandfather?"

"Shh, my love. You must go." His grip was implacable and his face stern, but he shivered.

"What are you doing? Where are you taking me, Grandfather?"

They moved rapidly through the village they'd visited to sell their wares just that morning, and for the first time since they'd arrived in the market place she felt fear. What was wrong? Was it something to do with Vasya?

"You are in danger. We must send you away." The words confused her further. Send her away? Danger?

"Where is Vasya?" She stumbled over a stone, but he kept tugging her onwards.

With a quick glance around, he hauled her into a dirty laneway between the buildings. Kira gasped, trying to drag air into her starving lungs. "There's no time. We must get you away."

A nondescript shopfront lay ahead, and he pushed on the door. It rattled and opened with a loud groan. "Andre? Andre, are you here?"

An older man shuffled into the room, bent nearly double from the weight of the load on his back. "Marat? What do you want?"

"My granddaughter. They are coming for her and us. Get her away. Take her now, while you can."

The man's face clouded over. "Are you sure?"

"Grandfather, where is Vasya?" Fright had the blood in her veins pounding.

"Hush, my precious. Andre will see you well." He turned. "Whatever it takes, Andre. Take her now." With surprising speed, her grandfather whirled and was gone.

The man, Andre, eyed her. "Come this way, child. There is no time to be lost."

Eleven years later

The tattoo of her heart and cry of terror woke her, as they usually did. Once again, as she had since that rapid flight from those who sought her, she found herself in a lonely bed. Hundreds of miles away from everything she'd dreamed of, in a house she'd built for them to share. As always, it left her wishing that Vasya had fled with her.

Instead, here she was, exiled without her husband. With a sob, she rolled over and let the tears fall.

Available from Beachwalk Press
books2read.com/IOTB

Direct Autographed Copy
http://bit.ly/2w6g4K6

The Celtic Cupid Trilogy

When Cupid—otherwise known as Diocail— is banished from his home on a remote Scottish Island, he's set a series of tasks by the great god Lugh, who also happens to be his father.

In **Blame The Wine**, he must bring two lovers together... BBW Cara and James, the man she's lusted over from afar who happens to be a super geek and head Veha Industries.

In **A Stranger's Embrace**, Diocail is driven to help an

emotionally fragile Jane and Davis, a famous author. The task is more complicated, with the existence of Carstairs her could-be ex-husband and teenage daughter, Frannie.

In **Revenge on Cupid**, Diocail must take the ultimate chance and find his own happily ever after with Simone. Sometimes the past gets in the way and HEA's don't come cheap though.

The dusty, dingy little diner was full, even with its current state of cleanliness—or lack thereof. People from the surrounding offices didn't care about anything except the incredible, well-prepared food at a reasonable cost. They flooded in, like waves to the shore. As one tide left, another swept in.

"Honestly, Simone. I'm going to try getting his attention one more time. If that doesn't work, I'm out of there. I mean, how long can I keep trying?" Cara picked at the caramel tart she hadn't been able to resist with the cheap metal fork and flicked the blob of fresh cream that sat on top to the side of the plate.

"You've said that tons of times before. Besides, what are you going to do to get his attention? Hmm? Walk naked through the typing pool?" Simone bobbed the straw in her smoothie as she eyed her friend with a frown. "It's been what? Eighteen months since you saw him, and you've mooned over him from a distance ever since you met him. You need to move on, Cara. That is, unless there's something you haven't shared?"

The query was arch. Cara shivered even as she shook her head. "No."

Simone quirked an eyebrow, obviously unconvinced with the answer. Cara let out a deep sigh of frustration. "There's a position...it's only temporary, for a PA reporting directly to him." She speared a forkful of tart, chewed quickly and swallowed, before continuing. "In his office, full-time for the period of the engagement. I saw the memo yesterday. I mean, I have the skills, right? I can type, answer phones, make coffee, file, greet people. What's more, I can probably do it better than all those size eights in the typing pool that Ms. Jackman seems to prefer." She nodded thoughtfully. "All I have to do is get past the ogre in Human Resources."

Simone stared at her, disbelief clear on her face. "Girl, I so remember that woman. If you think you can get past her, you're doing better than I ever did. That's why I left Veha Industries, remember? Maybe it's time to haul out your resumé and consider some other options. Look for something better." Simone shook her head and billows of her crimson hair swirled through the still air.

Cara understood Simone only had her best interests at heart. But this time she knew the outcome would be different. Hell, she could feel it in the air. The tingle of expectation.

"Cara, the HR ogre will hang you out for breakfast before she offers you anything like a position in that office. Remember her mantra? Good looks and good work make for a positive workplace!"

Simone didn't sugar-coat anything. It was another great reason for their long- term friendship. Honesty. But Cara didn't want to hear the truth in the statement. Even if it was exactly as her friend said.

Cara nodded quickly. "Yeah, I know, but if I don't try, then I won't know how close I can get to him, right? And the only way to catch his attention is to get past *her* and see him in person." Cara quaked a little at the information she needed to share. The favor she needed to ask. "Anyway, I tidied up my resumé and dropped the application into a memo envelope yesterday, so it's too late to back out now. I mean, fortune favors the brave. Doesn't it? If I don't snag an interview, I'm going to visit the career advisor across the street and register with them." She shrugged. "I'll look for temp work until something more long-term shows up. I can see what they have on offer and well...who knows? Maybe a job with the right boss is just waiting for me. But I'd rather this worked out, to be honest." Her voice trailed off into a whisper. "I really wish he would notice me."

Simone took a long slurp of her banana drink, and Cara noticed her questioning gaze even as she squirmed. Finally, Simone nodded. "It's your funeral. So anyway, you'd better show me this memo if you want me to be a referee for you. I'm guessing that's what you need, right? I'll have to know what I'm supposed to say about you before they ring."

Cara smiled. "Thanks, Simone. I knew I could count on you." She slipped a piece of paper out of her handbag and handed it over. "Sorry it's a bit creased. It was in the bottom of my bag, I stashed it so none of the others from the pool would see. You know how it is."

Available from Love Books Publishing
books2read.com/CelticCupid

Direct Autographed Copy
http://bit.ly/2vs7wtS

BioCybe by Imogene Nix

Can a cyber-enhanced warrior and a ship's captain find love together?

Levia Endrado never wanted to be a warrior, but at seventeen she was deemed suitable for battle. After intense training and multiple enhancements, which gave her superior strength and healing ability, she was sent off to defeat the enemy—a killing machine with a mission.

When the war was over, she had to find a new life. At twenty-seven she's a washed-up veteran without a future. Or she was, until she met Sandon Daria.

Serving as a pilot aboard Sandon's spaceship the *Golden Echo* makes Levia long for a different and gentler life. But old hurts and even older enemies aren't so easily forgotten. Particularly when they come back for her.

Sandon is determined to show Levia that she's more than just a BioCybe…she's the woman who completes him. Getting close is just the first step, keeping her alive is an even bigger challenge, but one he's willing to take because the prize is their combined future.

Levia scanned the long line of other hopefuls entering the chamber. The large building in the center of town was cold, and she dragged her wrap around her body, even as she craned her head, looking to the high ceiling. She'd never before had an occasion to enter the testing complex, yet she'd seen the lines of teenagers every time they passed the building.

Once she'd asked her parents why the teens were lined up and her mother's face had shuttered. Her stepfather had just shaken his head and growled. They'd stopped her questions with a carefully uttered, "You'll know soon enough, Levia." The pain in her mother's eyes had been enough to shush her questions. For endless months afterward, her parents had traveled different routes to the educational facility she attended and Levia lost interest in the puzzle of that building.

Now, as she looked around, remembering that long ago spring day, it was her opportunity to find out. But she felt a surge of concern at what lay ahead. She likely wasn't the only one, given that there were probably two to three hundred seventeen-year-olds gathered in the one place. Ahead of her, she caught sight of a couple of girls, their arms linked together and wide smiles on their faces.

Scanning the crowd, she became aware that, by far, a majority of those gathered displayed both fear and trepidation.

"All female subjects will enter through doors three, six, and seven. All male subjects will enter through gates four, eight, and ten." The speaker above her was loud, and she jumped before checking the numbers etched on the black metal sign over her head.

The massive doors beside her swung open, and now an uncertain silence reigned. Many of the youngsters hung back, clearly discomforted by whatever testing regime lay ahead. This was where they'd been told their futures would be determined.

"Oh gosh, I hope they only have an aptitude and psych eval. I don't think..." Levia turned to see the white face of the girl behind her. The girl had uttered what many must silently be thinking.

Levia dragged an unsteady breath in, her hand resting flat against the plane of her belly as she looked around. No one had entered yet. It was clear many were on the verge of taking the step, but still they hung back.

She straightened her shoulders. "I'm not afraid." It was always wiser to approach things head-on, she believed. When her biological father had died, she'd been one of the few to view his capsule before it was sent into the massive gray structure built to accommodate those who'd moved onto the next life realm.

Her legs shook as she wobbled toward the entrance. Beyond the doorway, she spied sealed cubicles and her heart stuttered. Why cubicles? Usually testing—med and psych—were in eval-units, hidden only by billowing white curtains. She glanced back, noting that others had taken the first step.

"Move along, subjects." Once again, the androgynous voice of the address system blared.

Of course, given it was her seventeenth anniversary of birth, she was technically considered an adult now.

She thought longingly of baby Rald and her half-sister, Elda, waiting at home for her to return, and the celebrations to be held that night. That made her smile. She would need to make them proud of her.

She entered a row and the tall Educational Specialist, the edu-specs as her peers laughingly called them, stopped her. "Present your credentials to the scanner."

She'd done this many times since the tiny implant had been slipped below the dermal layer of her skin at birth. The small unit in her wrist heated as her details were checked.

"Enter the first cubicle, Levia Endrado, and follow the instructions to complete your assessment."

Thus dismissed, Levia moved to the first unit, laid her palm against the scanner, and the door slid open soundlessly.

"Welcome, Levia Endrado. Take your place in the eval-unit." The soft contralto of the voice echoed after the door closed silently behind her.

"What are you evaluating?" Her voice was breathy, and she peered around.

"Your skills—physical and psychological. Your emotional and medical status. Your educational attainment levels."

It was an answer that shed little insight into the many things she was hungry to know. "Why do all seventeen year olds—"

"Take a seat, Levia. Then we may begin your testing."

If she'd expected an answer, she was sadly mistaken, she considered sourly. She dropped into the seat, the soft leather-like surface molding to her body.

"Levia Endrado, you are required to remove all non-specified apparel."

She jolted in the chair. "It's cold."

"The temperature will be amended. Remove the non-specified apparel."

Her misgivings grew as she dragged off the light wrap she'd brought with her, and then threw it to the floor at the side of the unit.

"We will begin, Levia Endrado. At any time, should you experience any malfunctions of the unit, simply depress the red button." It glowed and she grimaced.

Levia reclined against the chair and waited for the testing to begin.

The first examination was based on her understanding of the

political system, where she saw herself, and her knowledge of the rights and responsibilities accorded through citizenship of both her planet and the commonwealth.

The second test was mathematical and scientific proficiency. It felt like hours had passed by the time she'd finished, and she lay limp on the seat, exhausted.

"Levia Endrado, you may rise. The sanitary unit will emerge once you trigger the yellow button at the door. Should you require refreshment, press the blue button and a restorative will be made available."

"Can I leave?"

"Negative, Levia Endrado. Your needs will be catered for in this capsule."

"Why?" Her voice hitched and true fear rose for the first time. Why did they keep her in the alcove?

"All will be revealed at the end of the testing cycle."

Levia looked at the now empty screen before hurling a curse word. It was met with silence.

The urgent throb of her bladder reminded her that she needed to use the facilities, so, with

a sigh, she rose and clambered from the seat. After attending to the needs of her body, she walked around the unit, peering at the door, but it was obviously programmed remotely. She poked and prodded, but it made no difference. With a huff, she headed back to the chair.

The moment she'd settled in, the viewing screen shone bright. "Welcome back, Levia. The next sequence will evaluate your psychological reflexes, then that will be followed up with the general knowledge portion of the evaluation."

"When can I leave?" It seemed better to ask bluntly, she told herself.

"Once the examination is completed. After the next set of evaluations, you will be subjected to the physical aspect."

"Then I can go home?"

"Levia Endrado, you will now complete the psychological test. This will be undertaken by one of the center's personal evaluators."

She frowned. Personal evaluators? She bit her lip, and the sting reminded her that this wasn't something to joke about. In her seventeen years, she'd only heard of personal evaluators being brought in once before, and that was when one of the girls at her academy had been in a serious accident. Both legs were amputated and her body's ability to keep her alive had been gravely compromised. Her peers had been informed that the girl had requested the assessment before she could request her support systems be disconnected.

"Levia Endrado, are you ready to recommence processing?" The emotionless voice echoed once more and she gulped.

"Yes."

Available from Beachwalk Press
http://www.beachwalkpress.com

Direct Autographed Books
http://bit.ly/BioCybe

Also by Imogene Nix

Warriors of the Elector

- Star of Ishtar
- Starline
- Starfire
- Star of the Fleet
- Starburst
- The Star of Eternity

The Star of Ishtar & Starline - Print

Starfire & Star of the Fleet - Print

Starburst & The Star of Eternity - Print

Blood Secrets (Re-releasing 2020)

- The Blood Bride
- The Illuminated Witch
- The Sorcerer's Touch

The Search Duology

- Miss Elspeth's Desire
- Miss Isabelle's Craving (Not Yet Released)

Reunion Trilogy

- War's End
- The Assassin
- Executing Justice

The Reunion Trilogy in Paperback

Sex Love & Aliens

- Tangled Webs
- False Webs
- Covert Webs

21st Testing Protocol

- Cyborg: Redux
- Children Of A Greater Evil (Not Yet Released)
- When Evil Came To Stay (Not Yet Released)
- Finis: The War To End All Wars (Not Yet Released)

Celtic Cupid Trilogy

- Blame The Wine
- A Stranger's Embrace
- Revenge On Cupid

The Celtic Cupid Trilogy in Paperback (August 2019)

Zombieology

- The Reset (2018)
- I Dream of Zombies
- The Six Million Dollar Zombie (Not Yet Released)

Single Titles

The Chocolate Affair

A Sapphire for Karina

BioCybe

Hesparia's Tears

Tomorrow's Promise

A Bar In Paris

Inheritance Of The Blood

The Plan

Loving Memories

Hero of Heartbreak Hill

Raspberry Dreams (Not Yet Released)

Non Fiction

Self Publishing: Absolute Beginners Guide (With Suzi Love)

Written as Ciara Cave

25 Curated Ways To Get Rid Of Telemarketers

Book Signings for Absolute Beginners

About the Author

Imogene is published in a range of romance genres including Paranormal, Science Fiction and Contemporary. She is mainly published in the UK and USA.

In 2010, Imogene Nix (the pen name not Imogene herself) was born. Imogene sat down and worked tirelessly for 3 months culminating in the book Starline, which became the first in a trilogy titled, "Warriors of the Elector." Since then she's had over 30 titles published and is now focusing on hybridising herself - with a mixture of traditionally published and self-published works.

In fact, she's taking control of many of her back catalogue books, which are slowly re-releasing as self-published titles.

Imogene is a member of a range of professional organisations world wide, and believes in the mantra of mentoring and paying it forward and is actively involved in mentorship (through NaNoWrimo and her vlog: In The Chair With Imogene Nix) and tutoring of new and upcoming authors.

In her spare time she loves to drink coffee, wine & eat chocolate and is parenting her spoiled dog and a ferocious cat along with her husband and 2 human daughters and looks forward to weekends away with her husband in their caravan "The Seven Year Hitch!" Do look forward to her caravan romance at some point!

To Contact Imogene

www.imogenenix.net
imogene@imogenenix.net

f facebook.com/ImogeneNix
🐦 twitter.com/ImogeneNix
📷 instagram.com/ImogeneNix